A BODY
IN THE
VILLAGE
HALL

BOOKS BY DEE MACDONALD

The Runaway Wife
The Getaway Girls
The Silver Ladies of Penny Lane
The Golden Oldies Guesthouse

A BODY
IN THE
VILLAGE
HALL

DEE MACDONALD

Bookouture

Published by Bookouture in 2020

An imprint of Storyfire Ltd.
Carmelite House
50 Victoria Embankment
London EC4Y 0DZ

www.bookouture.com

ISBN: 978-1-83888-206-8
eBook ISBN: 978-1-83888-205-1

1

Kate Palmer struggled to keep awake as the 'Grow your own vegetables' woman droned on and on. She'd begun her lecture with beans – covered at length and clearly her passion – and she'd now got to brassica. 'That's your cabbage and your broccoli, ladies,' she explained to the less initiated members of the Tinworthy Women's Institute. Kate, sitting near the back on one of the highly uncomfortable chairs, decided that, in an effort to stay awake, she'd try to count all the women she recognised from behind. She'd only lived in Lower Tinworthy for around six weeks but she'd met quite a few of them on account of their bumps, lumps, arthritis and other assorted conditions, which came with the territory when you worked in the village medical centre. This was such a contrast to the life she'd led in West London. She'd moved to Cornwall with her sister, Angie, to get away from the hustle and bustle of the city. It had been the location of many idyllic childhood holidays and they'd always loved it here. Kate hoped fervently that living in such a tranquil location would give Angie some measure of rehabilitation from the demon drink, gin in particular. Hence the Women's Institute meeting; Kate was determined her sister would find something wholesome with which to fill her time.

Kate looked round at the rustic wood-panelled interior of Tinworthy Village Hall and at the collection of notices displayed. She could decipher the Gardeners' Club, Mothers and Infants, Tinworthy Train Enthusiasts, the Dramatic Society and the Over-Sixties' Club, none of which seemed particularly relevant. The Women's Institute – that backbone of rural life – wasn't exactly her cup of tea either, but she'd been hopeful that her sister might become interested. She glanced at Angie sitting alongside and decided that probably hadn't been such a brilliant idea, as Angie was fiddling with her phone and paying no attention whatsoever to the lady speaker and her brassica.

'Now, when it comes to your carrots,' the speaker continued, 'you should always—'

The ladies of Upper, Middle and Lower Tinworthy were never to know what they should always do with their carrots.

Suddenly, the speaker was cut off by a piercing scream. It came from the kitchen area at the back of the village hall.

There was a moment of complete shocked silence.

'What on earth was *that*?' Angie whispered.

Then chairs were scraped back in the general stampede towards the corridor that led to the kitchen.

'Kate Palmer!' someone yelled. 'Come here quick! We need a nurse!'

Kate pushed her way through the throng of women to the kitchen doorway. Betty Calder was half standing, half slumped against the doorframe. She looked like she was about to collapse, her face floury white. She raised a quivering arm and pointed wordlessly through the half-open doorway. Kate looked past her to get sight of what she was pointing at and there, lying flat on the floor, with a large knife sticking out of her chest, was Fenella Barker-Jones, hygienically clad for cake-cutting in plastic apron and latex gloves. There was a growing pool of blood round her body.

'Someone call an ambulance and the police,' Kate yelled as she ran to Fenella. She felt for a pulse without expecting to find one and tore away the apron to better examine the wound. The expression on Fenella's face told Kate – who had thirty-six years' medical experience – that the poor woman was dead; she looked wide-eyed and horrified, as well she might. Fenella Barker-Jones! She who had won the cake-baking contest at the start of the evening (although everyone knew it was Mrs Tilley, her cook, who'd done the baking).

Fenella, the Women's Institute chairwoman, the doyenne of the amateur dramatic society, the leading light of the Conservative Club and respected member of the Tinworthy Parish Council! She who, only twenty minutes ago, had introduced the guest speaker before disappearing into the kitchen to sort out the refreshments. And now here she was, lifeless, on the wooden floor.

For a brief moment Kate was stunned, but then her training kicked in and she gathered herself together. As she bent over Fenella's body, it was obvious from the angle of the knife that it had gone straight through her heart. She'd seen many dead bodies in the course of her career, but never anything quite as dramatic as this. What disturbed her most of all was the look of total shock and disbelief in Fenella's wide-open eyes. At least death must have been instantaneous.

'Stand back!' she ordered as several of the women nosed forward.

They'd gathered around but most were too horrified to go near the victim. Some were phoning the police, the doctor, their husbands. Betty, who'd crept out to help Fenella in the kitchen, was slowly coming round, but another woman had passed out, a couple were openly weeping and most were staring open-mouthed in morbid fascination.

'Who the hell would do something like this?' one woman shouted at no one in particular.

'Plenty might have wanted to,' someone else replied, 'but who would *actually* stick a knife into her?'

'We've only had that knife a few weeks,' muttered a large lady with pink hair. 'And it was mighty expensive. I suppose she must have been slicing that cake of hers.'

'Don't be daft! How could she do *that* to herself just slicing the cake?'

Everyone's eyes swivelled to the tabletop where Fenella's beautiful cake had been arranged into tidy overlapping slices, ready to be served with the post-talk tea.

'I think I'm going to be sick,' Betty Calder said as she stood up shakily, assisted by several others, and started heading towards the outside door.

'Don't go out *there!*' someone shouted. 'He could still be *out* there! Be sick in the loo! There might be a serial killer on the loose!'

Kate reckoned that this was about to become the most memorable – certainly the most sensational – evening ever experienced by the Tinworthy WI.

Five minutes later the wail of the police siren and the ambulance could only just be heard above the frenzied chatter in the kitchen and shortly afterwards several uniformed policemen burst through the door, accompanied by a non-uniformed older man.

'Stand back!' The older man examined Fenella. 'Who found this lady?'

'Betty Calder got to the door first,' someone replied, 'but she fainted and now she's in the loo being sick. But it's Nurse Kate over there who's been in charge.' They all pointed in her direction.

'Detective Inspector Forrest,' he said to Kate as he dug out his card. He had close-cropped dark hair, sprinkled liberally with grey, and kindly brown eyes. And there seemed to be unmistakeable traces of an American accent. 'You're a nurse?'

'I'm Kate Palmer. And yes, I'm a nurse, working at the medical centre.'

Just then Dr Ross, the senior physician at the medical centre, arrived. The doctor, after a minute, turned to Kate and the detective. 'You don't need me to tell you that this woman's dead.'

'OK, Doctor, but we hoped you could give us more detail than that. What would you say was the time of death?' asked the detective.

He leaned carefully over the body. 'Not more than an hour ago.'

'*We* could have told you that! She only introduced the guest speaker an hour or so ago,' another woman shouted.

'What about the cake then?' A thin, elderly woman was gazing at the artistically arranged slices. 'Shame to let it go to waste.'

The detective stepped forward. 'This is now a crime scene. If all you ladies would be kind enough to go back into the hall and sit down,' he said. He definitely had an American accent.

Kate went over to Angie, who'd been hovering in the doorway and who was visibly shaken.

'Come on,' she said, shepherding her sister back into the large draughty hall where everyone was now trying to find their seats.

'My God!' exclaimed Angie. 'I thought we'd moved down to Cornwall to get *away* from knife crime! You look a bit shaky too, Kate.'

'Are you really surprised? I came to this WI meeting for *your* sake, to try to integrate you into the area, and I thought I could have a nice little doze while you were educated in the delights of growing your own vegetables. Don't forget I've been working all day.'

'I don't want to grow my own vegetables but I do need a bloody drink,' Angie murmured, trawling in the depths of her shoulder-bag.

'Don't tell me you've sneaked in some gin?'

'OK, I won't tell you.' Angie lifted out what appeared to be a bottle of Highland Spring Water, according to the label. 'Nice drop of Bombay Sapphire and a splash of tonic. Nectar!'

Kate shook her head in despair at her incorrigible sister while at the same time wishing she herself had a shot of brandy or something to steady her nerves. She was used to keeping calm in a crisis but she was never going to be able to forget the sight of the knife stuck through Fenella's heart, and all that *blood*.

The babble of conversation was deafening; most of the women were grouped and huddled in horrified conversation, panic still etched on their faces. Already there was a smell of fear and perspiration in the air. The military rows of hard, uncomfortable chairs had been hurriedly abandoned and were now completely out of alignment so nobody was sure where they'd been sitting. The guest speaker was packing up her vegetables and looked eager to escape.

How strange it was that Fenella should die in the very hall that her husband's money had built! Seymour Barker-Jones was a great benefactor of the village. The village hall was an impressive and attractive stone-clad building with a steeply pitched roof, even if the interior was lined with cheap tongue-and-groove cladding, its grubby wooden floor only polished up for the children's Christmas party (also paid for by Seymour) and the St Petroc's Day celebrations and dance.

Angie swigged from her bottle and wiped her lips. 'That detective inspector, or whatever he is, is rather dishy, don't you think?'

'I didn't notice,' Kate said truthfully. 'I honestly could hardly take my eyes off Fenella.'

'Poor woman,' remarked Angie. 'I wonder who she managed to upset?'

'From what I've heard, she's upset quite a few,' Kate said. 'I've seen her around, of course, but I've never had to deal with her so she was obviously quite healthy.'

'Not so healthy now,' said Angie, taking another swig just as the detective inspector entered the hall and headed towards the platform where the speaker was still frantically packing away the carrots and leeks.

'Your attention, please!' he bellowed. 'As you're well aware, a woman has been murdered this evening in the kitchen, *right next door*.' He paused for effect. 'My officers are combing the surrounding area looking for clues and will be here for quite some time. Now the first thing I need to know is if any of you were absent from this hall at the time Mrs Calder screamed – which was presumably shortly after the murder took place. I'm going to need all your names and contact numbers please. The constable will be coming round with a form for you to fill in with your name and number. I will be in touch with everyone over the next day or two to take a formal statement.'

'Sandra Miller was out there having a crafty fag,' a woman next to Kate shouted. She nudged Kate and whispered, 'She smokes like a chimney *and* – she winked – '*her* husband's been having it off with Fenella for *years*. *Nothing* would surprise me…'

'I never thought I'd be leaving a building cordoned off with police tape,' Kate said as they emerged into the dark, damp night air and headed towards her red Fiat Punto.

'And whose bright idea exactly was it to retire down here and then join the bloody Women's Institute?' Angie asked as she got into the passenger seat and locked the door.

'Well, you were all for it too, Angie. After all, we've been here six weeks now. I felt it'd be good for you to meet people and get involved in village affairs since you're at home most of the time.'

'This was some initiation! And I still haven't a clue how to grow a carrot!'

Kate shuddered. 'I'll never forget that *look* in her eyes! It's the stuff of nightmares.'

'How old do you think she is? Was?'

'Around sixty I'd guess.'

As they turned out of the car park Angie said, 'Let's get home quick! I'm glad we're not walking tonight like you wanted us to! I don't feel safe with a maniac out there.'

'Well, I thought we needed the exercise, but I must admit I'm glad we're driving now,' Kate replied. She'd been thinking along much the same lines and was relieved to see so many police in the car park and here on the lane leading to the main road through the village. But her sense of unease returned as she headed down through the dark night to Lower Tinworthy and up the unlit winding lane to Lavender Cottage.

'Park as close as you can to the door,' ordered Angie, taking another hefty swig from her bottle, 'in case he's around somewhere.'

'Don't be ridiculous!' Kate got out of the car and headed towards the door. 'Why would he or she come down here?'

'Well, why would anyone want to kill Fenella? It could be some random opportunist killer who could strike anywhere.'

'I think you're safe here. The dog would be barking his head off otherwise,' Kate said as she fished out her keys.

As if on cue their springer spaniel, Barney, started barking. 'It's only because he's heard my key in the door,' Kate said. She locked the door carefully behind her, patted the dog on the head and said to Angie, 'You go check on the locks upstairs and I'll check down here.' As she spoke Kate remembered that the lock on her own bedroom window was non-existent; something else that needed fixing.

The house was pleasantly warm thanks to the log burner and the oil-fired central heating they'd had installed before they moved in. That, and replacing the rotten floorboards in the kitchen, had drained what little was left in their respective bank accounts, and necessitated Kate having to work three days a week as a practice nurse at the local medical centre.

Angie, who'd been a not-very-successful actress in her day, had taken up what she fondly called abstract painting, and commandeered the pretty summerhouse at the top of the garden as her 'studio'. Kate was not at all convinced that there was much prospect of income from Angie's random daubs, splashes and zigzags of paint.

'Oh God, I have to work in the morning,' she sighed as she collapsed into an armchair, clutching a large brandy with one hand and stroking Barney with the other. She'd always wanted a dog but she'd got Barney from a rescue centre mainly for Angie's benefit, in the hope that she would take him for walks and adopt a healthier lifestyle. In the six weeks they'd lived there, Angie had taken Barney for exactly two walks, so Kate wasn't overly hopeful.

'Will they *expect* you to work tomorrow after all this?' Angie asked.

'Of course they will! People aren't going to stop needing medical attention just because there's been a murder. I only hope I'm able to sleep.'

Kate tossed and turned and listened to her gin-sodden sister snoring away through the wall in the bedroom next door. That much-needed brandy had done little to obliterate the image of Fenella Barker-Jones lying in her own blood, her blonde coiffure still immaculate, that look of surprised horror in her eyes. She was also well aware that there was a killer out there somewhere but, hopefully, not in Lower Tinworthy. Kate couldn't for a single moment imagine any of her nice elderly neighbours, or anyone she'd met so far at the medical centre, being murderous types. But Kate also knew, from watching her favourite crime programmes on TV, that appearances could indeed be deceptive.

One of the things she found most stimulating about her work as a nurse was the 'detective skills' involved in figuring out the conditions people were suffering from and the clues their symptoms provided. But most of all she was fascinated by the human mind. She had done several psychology courses, primarily because it helped in her role of counselling patients, and it was the part of her work she loved and found most satisfying. At the same time it also fed her fascination with the human psyche. What made people commit such terrible crimes? Up until now her interest in the criminal mind had been sated by books and TV crime drama. In fact, watching the likes of *Morse*, *Midsomer Murders* and *Miss Marple* were her main sources of relaxation after the stresses of a busy day. But now she was in the middle of a real-life murder mystery! She never could have imagined that she would find herself in such a situation in a quiet Cornish village. It seemed that Tinworthy wasn't the gentle place she'd first thought.

The village of Tinworthy was divided into three: Lower Tinworthy was where they lived and Middle Tinworthy, which was half a mile up the winding road, housed the school, the medical centre and the large village hall in which most local events took place, including the WI meetings, as well as a large sprawling housing estate.

Kate had fallen in love with the pretty seaside village with its ancient bridge across the River Pol, the beach, the cliffs and the pastel-coloured houses clustered up the steep slopes on either side. There was a pub, several cafés, a small convenience store, a gallery and a few tourist shops. Kate had found Lavender Cottage on the internet while she was still up in West London. It was actually painted a pale-yellow colour, but it did have a whole hedge of lavender. It was also well above the river and the tourists, had sea views and was just about affordable. Kate had been divorced for twenty-eight years, Angie had been widowed for five years, and so they had decided to pool their resources, and head south-west. And now here they were.

A further half mile inwards and upwards was Higher Tinworthy with its farms, distant sea views and large houses, including Pendorian Manor where Fenella and her illustrious husband had resided. Kate had heard a lot about Fenella since she'd arrived in Lower Tinworthy. 'She liked the men' they said; she 'put it about a bit'. Her husband, Seymour, was a senior civil servant who spent most of his time in London. He was *very important*, everyone said, tapping their noses, and had apparently been invited to join the government. He appeared in Upper Tinworthy only for the occasional weekend and for Christmas, she was told. 'They say he's bisexual,' Sue, one of the other practice nurses, had informed her with some glee. 'They reckon he only married Fenella to appear respectable. Not that Fenella cares; she's got that whacking great house, and her horse and everything. And half the men around,' she added darkly. 'Anyway, Seymour's got pots of money; his grandfather, great-grandfather or somebody made a fortune out of tin-mining and they've been investing their dosh in all the right places ever since. Pendorian Manor's been in the family for generations.'

Kate had seen stab victims before when she'd nursed in London, but hadn't expected to come across much crime down here. She'd thought briefly that she might be able to retire when she and Angie decided to buy the cottage, described by the agent as 'picture-postcard perfect, on the hillside, 100 yards from the sea in a picturesque Cornish village'. They'd both fallen in love with its quirky nooks and crannies, its beams, its two steps down to the kitchen and three steps up to the sitting room, which came complete with inglenook and sea view. The spacious kitchen had been added on to the rear of the cottage at some point, and was separated from the sitting room by a large archway, which gave an attractive open-plan effect. The only problem had been the steps from one room to the other, which had taken a bit of getting used to, particularly with a cup of coffee in each hand. The agent hadn't of course mentioned the rotten floorboards, the lack of central heating or the bedroom windows that needed replacing, one of which didn't close properly. Fortunately, it was then Kate heard that the local medical centre was looking for a part-time practice nurse and decided to apply. But now she rather wished that tomorrow wasn't a working day.

It was almost 2 a.m. before Kate finally drifted off to sleep.

2

Next morning Kate studied herself with a critical eye in the full-length mirror. She looked as weary as she felt. People frequently told her she didn't look fifty-seven but that was probably because of her still lustrous mop of auburn hair, which had very little grey in it yet. This morning she was trying to tie it up tidily but without much success.

She was on duty at eight thirty at the medical centre and, although her car was parked less than fifty yards from the house, she still looked around nervously as she locked the door behind her. She knew that regardless of what problems the patients presented with today, the conversation was liable to be all about Fenella Barker-Jones. She was almost certain there had never been a murder in any of the Tinworthy villages before, at least not in recent years. Kate felt an almost personal responsibility to find out as much as she could about Fenella, probably because she had been the first professional on the scene.

'Good morning, Kate!' Dr Ross, the senior partner who'd been on duty last night, was making himself a cup of coffee in the tiny staff kitchen-cum-restroom with its sagging brown leather sofa where old Dr Payne used to like taking a nap between surgeries. Andrew Ross was a tall, rangy Glaswegian of fifty-five who'd married a Cornish lady and been persuaded to move south. Since his hobby was mountain-climbing this had involved a certain amount of sacrifice on his part.

He stirred his coffee. 'What a to-do, eh?'

'Good morning, Andrew. I don't imagine you've had much sleep either.'

He tasted his coffee, made a face and added a spoonful of sugar. 'Not much,' he said, 'by the time I confirmed her death, waited for the ambulance to arrive and explained as well as I could to the husband why one thrust of a kitchen knife could do such an effective job, it was midnight. Then countless photos had to be taken before poor old Fenella was carted away.'

'So you got hold of the husband?'

'Yes, eventually, on his mobile. No reply on his London landline but that's because he got back here a couple of days ago.'

Kate had heard quite a lot about Seymour Barker-Jones. He was well liked and respected in the Tinworthys from being the main source of the funds for most of the village's community amenities. As well as the village hall where his wife had been murdered, he had also given the land for the village cricket pitch, stumped up the funds for the new scout hut and given a generous donation to the school to provide sports equipment. Kate had gleaned this information from village gossip in the short time she'd lived in Lower Tinworthy. However, she hadn't yet met the much-talked-about Seymour, because he spent so much time in London. She'd heard about their unconventional marriage, which people seemed to think suited them both admirably, although he must surely have known of his wife's dalliances. Was it possible he would react in such an extreme way at this late date? Husbands, of course, were always prime suspects.

'Do you think the person who murdered Fenella might have had some medical knowledge?' Kate wondered aloud. 'It seems odd that they could have positioned the knife so accurately, don't you think?'

He shrugged. 'Possibly, or it could just have been a stroke of good luck, if you could call it that. Anyway, I see the waiting room's already crowded so I must get started. And what's the bet that they're all more than usually aware of their well-being this morning? '

He was right. Sue, the other practice nurse, who had worked here for a long time and knew everyone, was bursting to tell Kate about all the dodgy people who might have had reason to murder Fenella. And there was an impressive list.

'It's very strange,' she said, 'that this should happen a couple of days after Kevin Barry comes back to the village again. Don't know how he could show his face round here after what he did.'

'Who's Kevin Barry?' Kate asked.

'He used to work for Fenella years ago. He was supposed to be a handyman or a chauffeur or something, but he was a bit more than that.' Sue nodded and winked knowingly. 'Not only was he having her off but they were bevvied up half the time, and high as kites.'

'My goodness,' said Kate.

'And he was drunk and high on drugs when he ploughed into poor little Lucy Grey, who was on her way home from the post office. Must be about ten years ago now. Lucy was only eight and her poor mother, Maureen, has never recovered. Her husband couldn't cope with it and scarpered. No one's seen the bugger since. So poor Maureen's all on her own on the estate; one of those houses in St Petroc's Road. Anyway, Kevin got done for it and sent down for fourteen years. *But* – here she paused for effect – 'apparently, he's got out for good behaviour or something and he's come back *here*. Now, why would he do that?'

'It does seem a bit strange,' Kate agreed, consulting her watch. She really should be seeing her first patient. She had a feeling this shift was going to last longer than six hours.

'*Think* about it,' ordered Sue as she returned reluctantly to her own treatment room.

When Kate consulted her list she saw that Maisie Booth was her first patient.

'Were you at the WI meeting last night?' Maisie asked as she hobbled in to have the dressing on her new knee changed. 'Wish

I'd been fit enough to go – it must have been horrific!' She sighed, her eyes wide with excitement. 'But I got a good idea who it was that done it.'

'Oh yes?' Kate said as she removed the existing bandage.

'Yes,' said Maisie. 'I know you haven't been here long so you won't know everybody yet. Have you met the Millers who own The Atlantic Hotel in Higher Tinworthy? No? Well, let me tell you that he, Ed Miller, has been having it off with Fenella Barker-Jones for *years*. Now, this wife of his has been at it too, but with the French chef. *That's* been going on a couple of years or more apparently but' – she leaned forward – 'the chef's taken off with some Polish woman he met in the pub and now Sandra's left on her own-eo and is *not* a happy bunny. She wasn't that bothered about Ed and Fenella before, but she is *now*! See, she's most likely humiliated that the chef's headed off, plus the fact that her husband's being shagging a woman who's *ten years older* than he is! What does that say about Sandra?'

'It doesn't quite follow that she's likely to murder someone though.'

'You don't know *Sandra Miller*! That woman has a devilish temper! She was done for assault a few years back; some waitress or someone made a pass at her fancy French chef and Sandra flattened her. *Flattened her!* And Betty Calder tells me that Sandra went out for a cigarette last night and it was ages before she came back. Work it out for yourself! You couldn't make it up!'

Poor Fenella, Kate thought. *How many people might have good reason to want to be rid of her? The first patient of the morning and already we're up to a couple of suspects!*

'That's true,' Kate agreed. 'Now, that dressing should be the last one you need, but do come back if you have any problems.'

'Oh, I will,' said Maisie. 'Now, you mark my words about Sandra Miller!'

*

The next patient was Mary Morrison from Higher Tinworthy. 'I'm here cos of my nerves,' she said as she collapsed onto the chair. 'I'm needin' more of them pills and they said you'd be able to give me a repeat prescription. I'm too scared to open my front door with a serious killer on the loose, an' I'm not goin' to be able to sleep a wink!'

'Well, we can't be sure it's a *serial* killer,' Kate said. 'It could just be somebody who didn't like Fenella.'

Mary leaned closer. 'And there'd be *plenty* of them!' She tapped her nose. ''Er was a *loose woman*, you know! You ain't been 'ere long, but take my word for it – there'd be a few 'usbands and wives round 'ere that would like to see 'er gone. And what about that 'usband of 'ers, eh? 'Ow long was he supposed to put up with all 'er goings-on? And 'im such an *important person*! 'E's up in London, you know, and don't come down that often. And who could blame 'im, tell me that? I reckon 'e'd 'ad enough and she was becomin' an embarrassment. I wouldn't blame 'im if he took a knife to 'er.' And with that she hobbled out the door.

Kate knew that most of what she was hearing was village gossip but nevertheless she was fascinated. Crime on television was one thing but, like it or not, this was the first time she'd ever been involved in a real-life murder.

All the appointments had overrun, as Kate suspected they would. Just as she was making her escape, Sue caught up with her in the car park.

'You'll *never* guess what I just overheard!' she squeaked, catching Kate's arm. 'I just heard Dr Ross talking to Dr Colwill and they were rabbiting on about Dickie Payne – that's Dr Payne who retired a while back. Nice old boy he was, but he'd been having an affair with Fenella for *years* and everyone knew that.'

As she stopped to draw breath Kate wondered how Fenella had found enough hours in the day, and night, for all these dalliances.

'Apparently, Dickie tried to end the affair because the poor man was knackered. He's not in his first youth you know – must be seventy if he's a day. Anyway, Fenella wasn't at all pleased and threatened to tell Clare, Dickie's wife. Now, Clare's been disabled for *years,* which is probably why he went to Fenella in the first place.'

'Surely,' Kate said, 'if this doctor had been with Fenella for all these years his wife would have *known* about it? I mean, everyone else seems to have known, don't they?'

'No, no, nobody would want her to know; a shock like that might kill her.'

'So are you saying that he's *another* suspect? I mean how long is this list of lovers?' Kate was doing a mental check: add Dr Dickie to her list. Could there possibly be more?

Sue laughed. 'You won't see anything better than this on the telly,' she shouted as she went back indoors.

3

Kate should have been home by three o'clock, but after she had run late at the surgery she found the narrow road from Middle Tinworthy down to Lower Tinworthy blocked by an Outside Broadcast truck and she was held up yet again. She was becoming increasingly aware that the three small villages were agog with a mixture of fear and excitement. Television crews were appearing from nowhere, newspaper reporters had arrived in droves, the pubs and shops were doing a roaring trade and the Tinworthys were finally on the national map. Fenella had given them their five minutes of fame.

It was half past four by the time she got through her sturdy golden oak front door, which the previous owners had fitted.

'I've hardly had a drink all day,' Angie announced as Kate came in, 'and I wondered if we could go up to Lidl's because apparently they've got a special offer on gin.'

Kate sank wearily onto the sofa. 'Angie, I'm exhausted. And I'm not getting in that car again tonight. There is absolutely no way I'm driving eleven miles to that supermarket and you aren't either because doubtless you've already had a couple, haven't you?'

'Only teeny-weeny ones,' Angie replied sulkily.

'When your bank account finally runs dry I am *not* going to be subsidising your drinking habits,' Kate said, knowing full well that George had left her well provided for and it would likely be a long time before Angie drank her bank account dry. 'Put the kettle on for a cup of tea, would you?' There were times when Kate got fed up of the responsibility of caring for her older sister, much as she loved her.

As Angie stomped down the steps into the newly floored kitchen, Kate could hear her filling the kettle with much more noise than was necessary.

'Tell you what, Angie: I'm knackered and I don't fancy cooking tonight. I don't suppose *you've* organised anything?'

Angie reappeared from the kitchen. 'Well, I *thought* we might have got something in the supermarket,' she snapped.

'I've a better idea. Why don't we wander down to the pub in an hour or so and we'll eat there? We can do the shopping tomorrow.'

Angie brightened visibly. 'Good idea,' she said.

Angie had had a drink problem even before the death of her husband. George Norton had died five years earlier when the stress of his high-powered banking career finally drove him to a sudden and fatal heart attack. It had devastated Angie and taken her nearly three years to get back to a point where she could socially function again, by which time any hopes of getting back on the stage had gone. Her acting career had frequently been nipped in the bud (and the pub) by appearing late for auditions and then forgetting her lines which, in turn, required further alcoholic comfort. The only reason she continued to get work over the years was because she'd been stunning to look at and she could hold an audience in a vice-like grip. When she remembered her lines there was no one to match her. Kate had tried in vain to get her to go to AA or some support group, but Angie flatly refused to admit that she had any kind of drink problem. Any time Kate mentioned her concern, Angie would settle for – grumpy as hell – one glass of wine with her evening meal. Once she'd felt she'd proved her point, she was then at liberty to go on a bender the next day. Having tried everything she could think of, Kate was now resigned to the fact that Angie was happy enough, could hold her drink reasonably well and, at the age of fifty-nine, was unlikely to change. But it was certainly necessary to keep an eye on her.

The telephone rang just as Kate had got up to change out of her uniform. She picked up the phone. 'Hello?'

She recognised the mellow American voice of the detective inspector she'd met the night before.

'May I speak to Mrs Kate Palmer, please?'

'Speaking,' said Kate, aware that her heart was beating a little faster and hoping that her voice hadn't squeaked.

'I'm talking to all the ladies who were at the WI last night. Would it be possible for you and your sister to come up to the station in order to answer a few questions?'

'Yes, of course! When?'

'Could you both be here at Launceston Police Station about seven this evening?'

Kate had had a day discussing it all, listening to the patients' endless chatter and their lists of suspects, and all she wanted to do now was relax with her feet up and have a pub meal and a glass or three of wine. But it would be interesting to get a professional perspective and, not least, she was looking forward to seeing the attractive American detective again.

'You are kidding!' Angie said to Kate. 'What the hell do they want with *us*? We were in the hall listening to that old crone rabbiting on about carrots.'

'I know, I know,' Kate replied, 'but they want us to go and that's that. We can stop by the pub on the way back.'

They set off up the narrow winding road from Lower Tinworthy to Middle and Higher Tinworthy on the road to Launceston, and Kate noticed the blossom coming on the blackthorn trees and the swathes of primroses coming into flower. It was all the more beautiful in the spring evening light.

*

Detective Inspector Forrest looked to be about sixty. Kate guessed he'd be around six feet tall, and he looked as tired as she felt.

'Very fanciable,' Angie commented as they sat in the waiting area with a horde of other women from the previous evening. She breathed in Kate's face. 'Would you know I'd had a gin?'

'Yes,' Kate replied, 'I would.'

Just at that moment Angie's name was called and she disappeared into the little office where the interviews were taking place. Five minutes later she emerged, eyes sparkling. 'Yes, I could really, *really* fancy that man,' she confirmed.

A few minutes later it was Kate's turn. The detective inspector shook her hand and signalled for her to be seated. Kate looked around at the stark walls painted in grey. It was obviously not a room intended to put a person at their ease. However, DI Forrest smiled at her and she began to relax a little.

'Before we begin,' he said, sounding a little weary, 'I *know* you were inside the hall at the time of the incident and I *know* you're not a suspect, but I have to ask you a few questions anyway. You were one of the first on the scene and you checked to see if Mrs Barker-Jones was still alive or not. What about Mrs Calder who, I understand, was the first person to enter the kitchen?'

'Well, I believe she'd gone out to help Fenella with the refreshments but she got as far as the door and screamed. She was quite faint by the time I reached her. I believe she's a very nervous little lady at the best of times.'

'Yes, we've already had a word with Mrs Calder. Now, can you be absolutely sure that Mrs Barker-Jones was in fact dead when you approached her?'

'Definitely,' said Kate.

'Can you recall hearing any other noises at all? A car pulling up, perhaps? A rustling in the trees? Footsteps outside? Anything?'

Kate shook her head. 'To be honest I was almost asleep. Growing vegetables isn't really my sort of thing.'

He grinned at her. 'OK, so did you notice anyone around or anything unusual as you entered the hall earlier?'

'Nothing at all.' No wonder the man looked exhausted; he must have got to bed very late, if at all, and now here he was having to spend the day interviewing, only to hear the same story over and over again.

'There's always the chance that somebody might just have heard or noticed *something* unusual,' he said. Then he cleared his throat. 'I believe you're the new nurse at the medical centre?'

'Yes, I am,' Kate replied. 'We only moved down here a few weeks ago so I'm still finding my way around.'

'Does it seem a little provincial?' he asked with a grin. Dear Lord, he *was* very attractive! Was it the brown eyes, the golden skin or what?

Kate laughed. 'Sometimes, but charmingly so, and I like it for all that.'

'I may have to interview you further, Mrs Palmer, in the coming days. I understand you've bought Lavender Cottage?'

'How did you know *that*?'

'I'm a detective,' he replied with a wink.

An hour later Kate and Angie finally got to the pub. The Greedy Gull was a three-minute walk down the lane from Lavender Cottage and, in Kate's opinion, much too convenient as far as Angie was concerned. The building itself was around three hundred years old, two storey, with a rag-slate roof, ivy-clad walls and leaded light windows. A collection of rustic tables and chairs had optimistically been left out over the winter, and doubtless would be occupied when the tourists arrived in force again in the coming weeks.

The landlord was in chatty mood; Des Pardoe was tall, skinny and almost completely bald on top, his remaining grey hair yanked back into a sparse ponytail. He looked pale and sad but was, Kate had discovered, quite a wit.

'Good evenin', ladies! What can I get you? A little gin and tonic for you, Angie?'

'Definitely,' said Angie, 'but not so little, if you please.'

'I'll have a glass of white, Pinot Grigio would be perfect,' Kate said, sitting up on a barstool.

The building was old, but not as ancient as The Tinners Arms up in Middle Tinworthy. Des had whitened the walls, blackened the beams, polished up the brass and had had a large blue and white seagull, a fish in its beak, painted on each side of the inglenook fireplace. Kate thought he'd done a good job. It was loved by the tourists but not so popular with the older locals who preferred their pubs to be darker and grimier, like The Tinners.

As he served the drinks Des said, 'What a business about poor old Fenella, eh?' He paused while they murmured agreement. 'Mind you, I've a good idea who did it.'

'You do?' asked Angie, while Kate held her breath.

'Yeah, Kevin Barry. He's back in the village again after all them years in jail.'

'What was he in jail for?' Angie asked.

'Ah, I keep forgettin' you've only been here for a short time.' He then repeated almost word for word the story Kate had heard earlier.

'He was up there, supposedly workin' for her, for a couple of years or so, and they did some partyin', I can tell you!' He'd finished polishing one glass and had stretched out to replace it on the shelf above the bar. 'They were drunk as skunks half the time and the other half they were stoned out their minds!' He reached across to the tray of freshly washed glasses to pick up another one to polish.

'Once poor old Seymour came home and found them both out for the count in bed. He went ballistic!'

Again, Kate wondered how Fenella had found enough hours in the day for all these affairs. 'I daresay he did,' she murmured.

'Then, to cap it all, one day around ten years or so ago,' Des continued, 'this Kevin, stoned and pissed, takes Fenella's Land Rover and drives down towards the village and ploughs into poor little Lucy Grey on her way to post a letter.'

'Oh my God!' Angie exclaimed.

'He got done for drivin' under the influence of just about everythin' you can think of and for killin' poor little Lucy. Her mother's never recovered.' He paused while he put the money in the till. 'He went to jail but apparently got out early for good behaviour. *Good behaviour!* That's a bloody first!'

'So why would he come back here?' Kate asked.

'I'll *tell* you why he came back here, because he's got a long-suffering girlfriend, that's why. Jess Davey – so he's probably moved in with her. Nobody else'd have him, would they? And don't it seem funny that a couple of days after *he* comes back *Fenella* gets murdered? I reckon he went to see Fenella, wanting his job back, and she sent him away with a flea in his ear so he decided to have his revenge. Stands to reason it must be him.'

'Well, if he's guilty he'll probably be miles away by now,' Angie remarked, draining her gin.

Des waved his finger and gave a knowing smile. 'Now, *here's* the thing: Kevin's still around! Saw him today, strollin' in and out the shops up in Middle Tee, like he owned the bloomin' place! Scrawny guy, he is, don't look like he could say boo to a goose!'

'And she seemed to be quite a tall lady,' Kate remarked thoughtfully.

Des tapped his nose. 'Makes no difference cos it's the *surprise* element, see! She weren't *expectin'* it! You'll be needin' a refill, Angie?'

'Definitely,' Angie agreed.

'But why would he come to the WI of all places?' Kate asked. 'Why didn't he just finish her off up at Pendorian Manor? Surely, if she lives by herself most of the time, that would be the obvious place?'

Des shrugged. 'Well, I hear Seymour's back at the moment and they got staff, you know.' He handed them a couple of menus. 'Lasagne's good.'

As they sipped their drinks and studied the menu Des said, 'Of course it *could* have been Seymour.'

'The husband?'

'Yeah, poor long-suffering bastard.' Des shook his head in mock despair. '*He* don't want her, but he don't want anyone else to have her either. Don't forget he's payin' for all her shenanigans. I hear that him and Kevin was havin' a drink in The Tinners that evenin' too, so they was all around. Could be any of them!'

Could one woman *really* antagonise so many people?

'I'd hate to be that dishy detective trying to work it all out,' Angie said, taking a large slurp of her drink. 'Where do you reckon *he's* from, Des?'

'He told me once he was from California. Don't know what brought him over here,' Des said, 'but he's been in this area for probably around five years now.'

Kate decided not to mention the fact that the dishy detective had seemed to know a fair bit about her. But perhaps that was understandable since she'd been one of the first on the scene. And not in a million years would she admit to Angie that she thought he was dishy too.

4

When Kate consulted her list the following morning she saw that her first patient was Maureen Grey. *Maureen Grey?* Yes, of course, this was the mother of Lucy, the girl who was killed by Kevin Barry ten years ago. She wondered briefly if Maureen knew of Kevin's return to the area.

Kate picked up Maureen's notes and headed out into the waiting room. 'Maureen Grey!' she called. Maureen stood up. She was around Kate's height of five feet eight, but thin and pale with rapidly greying hair. Kate could see that she'd been pretty once with her heart-shaped face and large blue eyes. She wore a shapeless beige coat and plainly wasn't at all interested in her appearance.

Kate led Maureen back into the treatment room. 'Hi! I'm Kate, the new practice nurse here, so we haven't met before. What can I do for you?' Kate smiled but Maureen's face remained impassive. As Maureen sat down in the chair beside the desk, Kate was struck by how exhausted Maureen looked, her blue eyes sad and dull. And no wonder; she couldn't imagine how she'd be able to go on living if anything so dreadful happened to either Tom or Jack, her two lovely sons.

'I'm supposed to have my blood pressure checked because of my tablets,' Maureen said, slipping off her coat and rolling up the grey sleeve of a tatty, much-washed Aran jumper.

'Right!' said Kate, wrapping the cuff round her arm. After a minute she said, 'Your blood pressure's a bit high.' She studied the computer screen. 'I see you're on antidepressants, Maureen. You don't mind if I call you Maureen, do you?'

Maureen shook her head.

'You appear to have been on these antidepressants for a long time. Haven't you?'

'Yes, I suppose I have. What does that matter?'

'I wondered if you'd ever considered trying anything else?'

'Like what?'

'Some sort of therapy; counselling perhaps?'

Maureen looked thunderous. 'Why would I?'

Kate cleared her throat and chose her words carefully. 'Well, I can understand you must have struggled with depression for a long time, but there are alternative ways to deal with it, you know. Have you thought about counselling?'

'Nobody can help!' Maureen all but spat out the words. 'What can anyone do? *You* can't bring back my Lucy, can you?'

'No, I can't, but I can listen. There comes a time when you have to acknowledge your anger and grief, to shout and cry and get it out of your system.'

'Do you think I *haven't* cried?' Maureen said angrily as she stood up and rolled down her sleeve. 'You've no bloody *idea* how much I've cried! And all I want from you is my repeat prescription!'

Kate decided to have one last try.'

'Look, I do home visits too. If nothing else maybe I could pop in for a cup of tea and a chat sometime?'

'I don't want to make you a cup of tea and have a chat. I just want my damned prescription! Anyway, what's it to you? Why would you bother? You've not long been here, have you?'

'Exactly! So I've no preconceived ideas. I don't listen to gossip and I wasn't around here when the tragedy happened.'

Kate saw Maureen soften a little. 'You're bloody persistent, aren't you?'

Kate grinned. 'Yup!'

With that Maureen picked up her prescription and was gone.

Well, there was a tiny bit of progress there, Kate thought, wondering if Maureen would ever contact her again, or if she should arrive on Maureen's doorstep and hope to be asked in. She cast her mind back to the many times she'd had to stand her corner, to insist that a patient needed a certain medicine or therapy. Her persistence had usually paid off.

Kate had only had time to glance briefly at Maureen's medical notes before the appointment, so she decided to have a more detailed look now. The record of her prescriptions went back for years and years – she scrolled down quickly until she got to 2009. The newly bereaved Maureen had had to be restrained from attacking Kevin Barry when he'd been found guilty of killing Lucy. She'd waited until he was being transferred from the court to a prison upcountry and had presumably chosen her moment very carefully because he was on view for a matter of minutes. She'd only managed to swing her handbag at his head and spit in his face before she was grabbed by the police escort. When she'd got home she'd attacked her husband with a *bread knife*. He had fortunately managed to overpower her. She was then sectioned under the Mental Health Act, spent six months at St Lawrence's in Bodmin and had been on strong medication ever since.

Kate was appalled. Sad, frail-looking Maureen had attacked two men, one of them her husband. The bread knife particularly horrified Kate, with memories of the knife stuck in Fenella's heart.

As she was getting ready to leave, Denise the receptionist was talking to Sue at the desk.

'You'll never guess *what*! Kevin Barry's been arrested for Fenella's murder!' Sue said with glee. 'I *told* you, didn't I?'

'Thank goodness *somebody's* been arrested,' Kate said. 'Presumably we can all sleep easier in our beds now.'

*

Feeling somewhat deflated, Kate arrived home to find the dog gazing at her sadly and wagging his tail hopefully. Plainly Barney had not yet been taken for a walk.

Kate sighed and made her way up to the summerhouse, which must now be called the studio. Angie, of course, had locked herself in and as Kate approached, she obviously saw the shadow and picked up Kate's enormous heavy copper-bottomed saucepan from the floor. Then, seeing it was her sister, she laid it down again as she unlocked the door.

'What on earth are you doing with that pan?' Kate asked.

'It's just in case the killer decides to call,' Angie said cheerfully, 'so I can bash him over the head.'

'But you're locked *inside*!'

'Yes, but it's not double-glazed, so he could easily smash the glass.'

'And why would he be so keen to do that? Why, of all the people in the Tinworthy villages, would he choose *you*?'

'Because I think he's a random serial killer, Kate, who probably hates women. Why else would he kill Fenella? He looked through the window, saw her in there on her own slicing the cake and decided he could put the knife to better use.'

'I take it then you've not heard about Kevin Barry being arrested?'

'Really? Well, he was supposed to be the favourite suspect, wasn't he? Still, I'll wait until they prove him guilty before I relax completely,' Angie said, as she daubed some purple paint over the green and yellow squiggles she'd already created.

Kate decided to change the subject. 'May I ask why you haven't taken our poor dog out for a walk this morning?'

'Apart from the fact I was likely to be *murdered*, do you mean? Well, I'm feeling really creative today and I have to work when the muse takes me.'

Kate groaned. 'The muse takes *me* to put my feet up and have a large mug of tea. Instead of which' – she consulted her watch – 'I now have to take Barney along the cliffs and get blown to bits by the wind.'

'Great for the complexion,' Angie retorted, 'and it will blow away all the germs you've acquired after being cooped up with all those unhealthy people.'

'I notice a distinct lack of concern about *me* being out on my own and minus a saucepan.'

'Well, I'm going in now, so you can take it with you if you want.'

The dog, in the meantime, was continuing to gaze up adoringly at Kate, his tail wagging.

'OK, Barney,' Kate said, 'I'll just change into my boots and then we'll be off.'

As Kate climbed the hill to the top of Penhallion Cliff and along the coastal path, she paused for a moment, as always, to listen to the sound of the waves crashing against the rocks beneath and the noise of the seagulls circling overhead.

From here she could look down to Lower Tinworthy and to the river meandering its way to the sea past the little parade of shops and tea rooms, which would be opening up again shortly for the season, whilst admiring Lavender Cottage on the hillside opposite. Directly across and further inland was Middle Tinworthy. She glimpsed a roof that might have been the medical centre, but she couldn't be sure. And there, at the top of the hill, was Higher Tinworthy, with Pendorian Manor and its neighbours looming over the scattering of new-build luxury houses and the lower villages.

'It'll be swarming with tourists,' she'd been warned by an old lady who lived further up the lane. 'They'll be looking in your windows like you're some sort of tourist attraction and taking photos left right and centre. Just you *wait*!'

Easter was now only a few weeks away, so Kate guessed they'd soon be arriving. In fact, she'd already spotted some early visitors bravely tackling the wind as they strolled along the beach, looking around hopefully for a café or something that might be open. Only The Locker Café opened in the early spring for a few hours.

'Somebody's got to look after them poor emmets!' Polly Lock said.

As Kate turned to continue her walk, she saw Barney, now off the lead, wild with excitement and jumping around with a couple of black Labradors who'd suddenly appeared. They were followed by a tall, slim, grey-haired, clean-shaven man, ruddy-cheeked and clad in a Barbour jacket and tweed cap, with his trousers tucked into long leather boots. He looked to be in his mid-sixties.

As he neared, Kate said cheerfully, 'Good afternoon! Rather windy today, isn't it?'

'It is,' he agreed politely, but he looked solemn.

Kate retrieved Barney by the collar. 'Sorry about him; he loves the company of other dogs.'

'Of course he does,' the stranger said. 'Dogs are very sociable. Are you a visitor?' He had that clipped speech so typical of the gentry.

'Oh no,' Kate said. 'But we haven't been here very long. We've bought a cottage down there.' She pointed down to Lower Tinworthy.

'Well,' he said, 'I hope you'll be very happy here.' He stretched out his hand. 'Seymour Barker-Jones.'

Kate gulped. Had she heard correctly? *Fenella's* husband?

'Kate Palmer,' she said, shaking his hand. 'Did you say Sey—'

'Yes,' he interrupted, 'Seymour Barker-Jones. I have a feeling you may have heard the name.'

Kate didn't quite know what to say. She hesitated for a moment, then said, 'I'm very sorry about your wife.'

Seymour Barker-Jones was shouting at one of his Labradors. 'Come *here*, Meg!' Meg reluctantly obeyed and he turned back towards Kate. 'Thank you,' he said before walking off hurriedly in the opposite direction.

Another suspect! He certainly didn't look like the bread-knife-wielding type, but then neither did Maureen.

Kate watched him for a moment. The famous – or was he *infamous?* – Seymour. He fitted perfectly Kate's preconceptions of what a senior civil servant would look like on his days off – pleasant, polite but not in the least bit exciting. Kate could well imagine why somebody with Fenella's reputation would need a more scintillating lifestyle. And Seymour looked like the type of man who would be happy to leave her to her own devices, his marriage having been, according to rumour, unconventional to say the least.

5

When she got home Angie was pouring herself 'the first gin of the evening', which Kate doubted as she observed the couple of empty tonic cans on the work surface.

'Enjoy your walk?' she asked as she bent to stroke the dog's head.

'You'll never guess who I met,' Kate said as she collapsed onto the sofa.

'Daniel Craig? George Clooney?'

'Just as interesting: Seymour Barker-Jones!'

Angie stared at her. 'You're kidding! Where?'

'Up on Penhallion, walking his dogs. Introduced himself. Seemed nice.'

'Kate, he might be the *murderer*!' Angie's eyes widened in horror.

'I thought I told you that Kevin Barry had been arrested? Anyway, he didn't look like a murderer to me; he was very pleasant and quite attractive. Posh accent. Typical English country gentleman, you know: tweed cap, Barbour, Labradors.'

'You sound quite smitten and, hey, you're in luck because he's a free man now, isn't he!'

Kate sighed. 'Of course I'm not *smitten*! We only spoke for a couple of minutes and when I said how sorry I was about his wife, he headed off in the opposite direction.'

'Perhaps he didn't fancy you. Or maybe so you couldn't see the guilty look on his face.'

Kate rolled her eyes. 'OK, next time I go I'll take the saucepan with me just in case I run into him again.'

*

After supper – during which Angie had imbibed more than her share of a bottle of wine – she said, 'I might just take a stroll along to The Greedy Gull in a minute. Feel like coming? There's not much on the telly tonight.'

Kate had rather fancied watching a re-run of *Midsomer Murders*, but she didn't think she should leave Angie to follow her own urges. She would most likely hit the gin and come home at all hours, much the worse for wear. Sighing, she wondered again if it had been such a brilliant idea to buy this place with her sister. She'd hoped that, in beautiful Cornwall, somehow or other their problems would disappear, or at least be diminished. She'd visualised Angie going for long walks with the dog and getting involved with local events. And just settling for a couple of drinks in the evening, like most people did.

The Greedy Gull was as far as Angie went most days. Des, of course, knew a good customer when he saw one, so consequently had done nothing to discourage her. In fact, they'd become quite chummy and Kate reckoned he probably fancied her because he kept giving her free drinks.

Both of Kate's sons had approved of the move to Cornwall in general, but had questioned her going with Angie. 'You *know* what Aunt Angie's like, Mum!' Yes, she did know what her older sister was like but she couldn't help feeling responsible for her. Their mother had always worried about Angie. 'She's got that gene your father had,' she'd informed Kate. 'Alcoholic.'

Now here they were in the bar – which was crowded this evening – and Angie had pushed her way through to where Des was already pouring her a gin.

He leaned across the bar towards them both. 'Look over *there*,' he ordered, wagging his head towards the inglenook.

'At what?' asked Angie, taking a sip of her neat gin before pouring the tonic in.

'*Kevin Barry!* Over there in the blue jacket, talkin' to Jess Davey, her with the black curly hair. The *cheek* of him! Wandering around like he hadn't just killed someone!'

'But I heard earlier that he'd been arrested,' Kate remarked, turning round to have a look.

'Remember I told you Kevin was chattin' to Seymour at The Tinners, that night?' Des leaned in a bit closer. 'But The Tinners is only a dozen yards away from the village hall so he could easily have nipped in there, shoved the knife in and been back in the bar in the time it would have taken to nip out for a fag! Now we got all them press and TV people comin' down, but where are they? Tell me *that*! How come they're all up in the bloody Tinners and not down here?'

'Perhaps the beer's cheaper?' Angie suggested.

'Not much cheaper it ain't. No, it's cos it's close to the village hall, scene of the murder and all that. Pity her didn't get murdered down here, no disrespect and all that…' Des sighed.

Kate stared hard at the man in the inglenook. From what she could see Kevin Barry appeared to be of average height, with short dark hair and a long nose. His most distinguishing feature was the deep scar that ran down his right cheek. He seemed completely unaware that several pairs of eyes were staring in his direction. The woman, Jess, had a dark complexion, with a selection of piercings and some sort of tattoo decorating her right arm.

'Well,' said Kate, 'he hasn't wasted any time in getting back with his girlfriend.'

'Ah well,' said Des, 'they was an item long before he went to prison and her stayed devoted to him all the time he was in there.

I'll say that much for her, her went to visit him every month, regular as the new moon! God only knows why her stuck by him when he was havin' his evil way with Fenella. Mind you, they do say Jess was putting it about a bit herself.'

Was it something in the water down here? Kate wondered. How come everybody was having it away with everyone else? For a small village it certainly had more than its share of goings-on. Not to mention a murder.

'So how come he's drinking in here?' Angie asked, taking a gulp of her gin.

'Well, I suppose there's no reason why he shouldn't,' Des said, staring openly at him. 'His money's as good as anyone else's. Innocent until proved guilty and all that. And I *do* think that bugger's going to be found guilty, alibi or no alibi. Otherwise why would Woody Forrest be in here keeping such a close eye on him?'

'Yes, you're right!' Angie was now nudging Kate fiercely. 'Look, *look*!'

'What?'

'The lovely detective! Over there near the door!'

Kate picked up her glass of wine and turned round to look towards the door. And there he was, Detective Inspector Forrest, talking to a younger, shorter man. At that exact moment he looked up, his eyes met Kate's, and he smiled. She smiled back.

'Hey, what's he smiling at *you* for?' Angie asked.

'Must be for my outstanding beauty and personality,' Kate said, sipping her wine.

'He's got nice teeth,' Angie muttered. 'Hope they're his own.'

As Angie turned to talk to the man next to her, Kate cast a surreptitious glance in the detective's direction – at the exact moment he was having a surreptitious glance in hers. Again he smiled and she wondered if he could see her blushing furiously. *I shan't look at him again*, she thought, wondering why she was acting like an overgrown adolescent.

She turned back to Angie who was chatting to someone called Luke who appeared to be in his forties and apparently owned The Gallery down by the river.

'Well, I'd certainly be interested in *seeing* your work,' said Luke sniffily, 'but of course I can't guarantee being able to stock it at the moment because I'm *inundated* with stuff.'

'This is my sister, Kate,' Angie said. 'Kate, this is Luke.'

'Hello, sister Kate,' said Luke, sweeping his luxuriant blond locks away from his eyes to behind his ears and exposing a collection of metalwork attached to his earlobe. Then, *sotto voce*: 'What about this *murder*, then?'

'It's certainly the main topic of conversation,' Kate said.

'Not a lot of that sort of thing happens around here as a rule,' Luke said. 'Certainly beats discussing Plymouth Argyle's chances of winning on Saturday!' He guffawed and looked at Angie's rapidly emptying glass. 'Can I get you another of those?'

'Most kind,' murmured Angie, handing him her glass. 'So who do *you* think did it?'

'Without a doubt, Sandra Miller,' he said, getting some cash out of his pocket. 'I'd put money on it. A woman scorned, and all that. Her husband's been having it off with a woman ten years older than he is and her French chef doesn't want her anymore. Wham, bam, thank you, ma'am! Sandra's rejected *again*! Now, she either finishes off her husband or his mistress but she knows which side her bread's buttered and she couldn't carry on with that hotel on her own. So Ed's off the hook.'

'But surely if she's put up with it for all these years – and everyone knows – it's a bit late in the day to do something about it *now?*' Kate said, remaining unconvinced.

'Ah yes, but I've heard they've been rowing a lot lately, ever since the Frenchman left. And she's got a fiendish temper, has Sandra. And I've been hearing she went outside for a smoke during that WI meeting and came back in ages later. She *couldn't* come back in until she cleaned herself up, see, because she'd be covered in blood, wouldn't she?'

'That's very unlikely,' Kate said thoughtfully. 'All the blood was underneath.'

Angie looked doubtful. 'But Des is *convinced* it's Kevin Barry.'

'Only because he's reappeared after all these years. Anyway, he's got an alibi so they've had to let him out. But Barry's OK. Yeah, I know he knocked down that little girl, but he was completely stoned at the time – it was an accident – and, let's face it, he's paid the price. I know he didn't serve the full sentence, but he was in there for around seven or eight years. He's a nice enough bloke; I was chatting to him earlier.'

'Kate here met Seymour on the coastal path today while she was walking the dog,' Angie remarked.

'Old Seymour? *He's* all right,' said Luke. 'He's a big shot up in London, you know. I wonder how he's coping with it all?'

'Well, I got the impression he was putting a brave face on things,' Kate remarked.

'Ah well, he's the stiff-upper-lip type. Probably doesn't want to talk about it anyway. Mind you, he hardly spent any time with Fenella, being up in London so often. Never seemed much bothered about her love affairs, but he *must* have known because everyone else did.'

Kate was becoming increasingly fascinated by the subject but she tired. 'Well, I'm ready to go home,' she said, taking the opportunity to get a word in edgeways and looking towards the door to where the detective was still deep in conversation.

'I fancy staying a bit longer,' said Angie. There was a whine in her voice.

'No, I don't think you should,' Kate said firmly. 'Have a nightcap at home, if you must. I'm not having you coming home late on your own.'

'Perhaps I should have brought the saucepan?'

'You probably should have,' Kate agreed, relieved to see her sister wasn't about to start arguing. 'Nice meeting you, Luke,' she added as she shepherded Angie towards the door.

'It's only half past nine,' Angie was muttering.

As they reached the exit the detective had to stand aside to let them pass.

'Good to see you again,' he said, smiling at Kate.

She smiled back, aware of a slight increase in her heartbeat.

6

By Saturday the initial shock and excitement had abated a little in the area. Angie had even replaced the saucepan in the kitchen. Kate spent the morning in B&Q and returned with some emulsion paint for her bedroom. She'd never realised there were quite so many variations of white, particularly as she'd once been taught that white was *not* a colour. *Well, it certainly was in B&Q, and the paint manufacturers must be making a fortune out of all their fancy whites*, she thought. Kate had finally decided on 'sunbeam white' and, in preparation, had begun to move the smaller items out of her bedroom and onto the landing, and then spread dustsheets over the bed and the floor. She was almost ready to begin – stepladder in position – when the dog appeared with *that look* in his eyes.

'It's Angie's turn to walk you today, Barney,' she said, wondering where her sister had got to. She called out, '*Angie!*'

No reply. Kate wondered if perhaps she'd gone out to do some of her artwork and decided to investigate before she prised the lid off the paint pot. But there was no sign of Angie anywhere. *She* can't *be*, Kate thought. *Surely she can't have sloped off to the pub* already*?* She looked at her watch: half-past one, lunchtime. There seemed little point in beginning to paint with Barney haunting her and so, feeling annoyed, she attached the lead to the dog's collar and set off for The Greedy Gull.

The pub was busy, being Saturday, and as Kate peered in the door it took her several seconds to spot her sister, on a barstool, surrounded by three men, one of whom was Luke.

Kate strode in, the dog at her heels. '*What* are you doing in here?' she asked Angie. 'You *promised* to walk Barney today so I could get on with painting.'

Angie looked up and Kate could see from her slightly unfocused eyes that she'd already had a few.

'I'll be home in a minute,' Angie said crossly. 'The dog can wait for a bit, surely? Let me introduce you to…' She hiccupped as she turned to a short man with a beard. 'I seem to have forgotten your name?'

'Don't bother!' Kate was angry. 'I can't rely on you to do a damned thing!' With that she turned around and she and the dog stomped out. Outside, she took a deep breath of sea air to calm herself down. This was one of the many occasions when her sister drove her crazy.

Angie was still an attractive woman with her big blue eyes and highlighted hair. But she'd put on weight and was now quite chubby, due in no small part to her endless consumption of gin and wine. As a teenager Angie had badgered their parents to send her to drama school because she was going to become a big star. Just you *wait*, said she. Eventually they gave in and off she went to drama school where she learned that acting wasn't just all about looking pretty and learning lines but was damned hard work. George Norton, her long-suffering husband, had let her get on with it, indulging her every whim and immersing himself in work to pay the bills.

When Jeremy was born, Angie took a couple of years off. Her son became her passion, her *raison d'être*. That is until he took off to Sweden to study anthropology and got himself a Swedish wife while he was about it. Angie did not like Ingrid, and the feeling appeared to be mutual. Nevertheless, she headed to Sweden for a week each year to where Jeremy and Ingrid lived in Scandi splendour on the edge of a lake in a village with an unpronounceable name near Malmö. Each year she swore she'd never go again. Her son had grown a beard and looked like a Viking, his tall, stunning, blonde wife openly disapproved of Angie's drinking habits and the whole family – including their two little boys – liked nothing better than tramping through forests and swimming in icy water.

Such was Angie's suspicion of all things Swedish that Kate was barely able to persuade her sister to go through the door of IKEA these days and frequently had to prevent her from kicking passing Volvos.

The dog needed a walk and Angie wasn't going to be doing it, so the painting of the bedroom would have to wait.

Kate couldn't face the cliffs today but she'd discovered there was a very pleasant route up by the churchyard in Middle Tinworthy. She set off up the hill for the thirty-minute walk up to the middle village, and both she and Barney were panting as they reached the top. They strolled past the medical centre and the school towards the ancient church of St Swithin, with its graveyard that straggled up the hill towards the woods behind, where Kate intended to go.

She decided to take the path round its old stone walls to reach the woods, and it was then that she heard the voices – raised voices, furious voices – coming from somewhere among the graves. Kate stood stock-still behind the wall and listened.

'What the hell do you want coming here? How *dare* you! They should have thrown away the key when they locked you up!' a furious female voice shouted. 'Go *away*!'

'Listen, Maureen,' a male voice shouted back, '*listen*! I've something to *tell* you!'

'I don't want to hear *anything* from you!'

Kate peered out from behind an escallonia bush and saw that the woman was – without a doubt – Maureen Grey. She appeared to be placing what looked like a posy of primroses on what must be Lucy's grave.

'But Maureen...' the man's voice wheedled.

'You've got *nothing* for me, nothing!' Maureen screeched. 'Don't you *dare* come near this grave! We don't want your bloody flowers!' She bent down and picked up a bunch of pink tulips and flung them towards the wall.

Kate could now make out the figure of Kevin Barry.

'You don't understand!' he said.

'Bloody right I don't!' Maureen picked up an urn and, raising it high, ran towards him, aiming at his head. Kevin moved quickly away and down the path. 'Didn't you get my letter?' he yelled back at her. 'And I got a recording now that proves it!'

'Makes no difference,' she snapped, laying down the urn. 'I don't care *who* was driving! You were in the car and off your head on alcohol and drugs.'

As Maureen turned back to the grave, she caught sight of Kate, who was moving slowly up the path by the wall. 'What are *you* looking at?'

'I'm not looking at anything,' Kate said, 'I'm just walking my dog.'

Kate watched Kevin walk away. He seemed deflated, dejected, defeated. She felt a little sorry for him and then wondered why. There was no good reason why she should and there was every good reason to feel sorry for Maureen. She hesitated for a moment then turned back towards the gate – dragging an unwilling Barney by the lead – and headed to where Maureen was kneeling on the ground, weeping silently.

'Maureen?'

Maureen looked up, wiping her eyes with the back of her hand. 'Oh, *you're* still here!'

'Yes, I'm still here.' Kate looked at the little white gravestone. 'When you're ready I'm going to walk home with you.'

'Why the hell would you do that?'

'Why? Because I'd like to chat with you. I can see you're angry and you don't want to have another breakdown.' *Or do someone harm*, she thought, looking down at the urn into which Maureen had now arranged her primroses.

Maureen shrugged and stood up. 'He had the gall to bring tulips to Lucy's grave.'

'Perhaps he meant well?'

'That man does *not* mean well,' Maureen snapped. 'He's an evil bastard.' She picked up the bottle of water and plastic bag she'd brought with the primroses. 'As are *all* men.'

'No, Maureen, they're not all bad. You've just had more than your share. You've been so unlucky.'

'Unlucky! Is *that* what you call it? I've had to face all this on my own, you know, thanks to a weak husband who couldn't cope and took off to God-knows-where.'

'Well,' said Kate, 'my husband took off too, but with another woman, and left me with two little boys.'

Maureen looked at her for a moment. 'But you still have your boys.'

'Yes, I still have my boys; one in Scotland, one in Australia, so I don't see them often.'

'But you still *have* them,' Maureen repeated, 'and you saw them grow up.' She began to walk slowly towards the gate.

Kate followed her down the stony path, the dog dragging on the lead. Outside the gate Maureen turned left and Kate fell into step alongside her. Nothing was said for a few moments until Maureen asked, 'What sort of dog is that?'

'He's a springer spaniel. His owner died and he was put into an animal shelter, which is where I found him. He's nine, and he's settled in well. His name is Barney.'

'Barney,' Maureen echoed. They continued walking in silence towards the housing estate. Kate knew Maureen lived in St Petroc's Road, which turned out to be near the western edge that they were now approaching. 'Don't suppose you've ever been on this estate before?' Maureen said.

'You're right, I haven't.'

Kate had heard there were some roads of detached houses on the estate but this wasn't one of them. St Petroc's Road consisted of a row of unlovely porridge-coloured pebble-dashed council semis. Maureen's house had a green-painted door and a well-polished brass knob and letter box. There was a plain strip of lawn to the front and a bicycle leaning against the wall.

'Is it OK to bring the dog inside?' Kate asked as Maureen unlocked the door. 'We won't stay long but I would love a cup of tea.'

Maureen directed Kate into what was plainly an unused sitting room and indicated, tight-lipped, that she should sit down on the uncomfortable-looking dark green leather sofa. Kate looked around. There was a wall of photographs: Lucy as a baby, as a toddler, on her first day of school, on the beach in a pink swimsuit, at some fancy-dress event where she was presumably a cat, clad in a furry suit with whiskers painted on her cheeks. The room was ice-cold.

Kate remained standing. 'I'm not some sort of honoured guest,' she said.

'That's right, you're not,' Maureen agreed.

'So I'm quite happy to join you in the kitchen or wherever you normally sit. And Barney certainly shouldn't be in here.'

Maureen didn't argue, just shrugged and said, 'OK, come through.' Maureen did a lot of shrugging. 'Through' led to a messy kitchen-cum-living room with a couple of sagging armchairs positioned on either side of a plain wooden fireplace containing an old two-bar electric fire. There was what looked like a half-knitted red jumper on one of the chairs. Kate noted there were no radiators so, presumably, there was no central heating. She couldn't imagine there was anything as up-to-date as underfloor heating.

Maureen bent down and switched on the fire, which began to warm up slowly, accompanied by the smell of burning dust. When had that fire last been on? Barney, who was no fool, immediately plonked himself down in front of this only source of heat, head on paws, whilst keeping a watchful eye on Kate.

As she watched Maureen fill the kettle, she said, '*I* was going to make *you* a cup of tea.'

'Why would you do that?'

'Because I don't suppose you get many cups of tea made for you,' Kate replied honestly.

'I go in to Brenda's next door sometimes,' Maureen said as she placed the kettle on the gas hob. 'I'm not a great socialiser.' She paused. 'No doubt you've heard that.'

'I don't pay a lot of attention to gossip,' Kate said. 'I like to make up my own mind.'

Maureen was dropping teabags into two mugs, then adding the boiling water. 'Milk? Sugar?'

'Just milk, please,' Kate replied, lowering herself into one of the armchairs and hoping Maureen wouldn't suggest she take off her coat.

Maureen handed her the mug of tea, sat down opposite and picked up her knitting. 'So, what are we supposed to talk about?'

'You're not *supposed* to talk about anything. I just thought you might like a chat. What was all that rumpus in the graveyard about? I mean, I know Kevin Barry killed your daughter but—'

'He *says* he didn't,' Maureen interrupted. 'He wrote me a letter while he was in jail telling me it was really Fenella who was driving. Now he says he's got proof. Like some sort of recording, he says. He says he's keeping it because he can use it against Seymour. He says he knows who killed Fenella, so I reckon he probably means Seymour.'

'Well, if he says he's got proof, shouldn't you let him show it to you?'

Maureen took a gulp of tea. 'You know what? I don't care what proof he's got because he and that bitch were in it together – always drunk and on drugs, no thought for anyone else.'

Kate felt desperately sorry for her. 'Don't you have anybody you can turn to, Maureen?'

'Not unless you count my so-called husband who's suddenly reappeared from nowhere! Came knocking on the door last Sunday, he did.'

Kate took a moment to digest this. 'Why would he come back now?'

'It was ten years to the day that Lucy had died and he said he'd been away too long. He asked me to forgive him – huh! Seems he got a letter from Kevin Barry too. Talking of which, if he hadn't sent Lucy down to post his bloody football coupon, she'd still be with us. He was wittering on about having some sort of breakdown but, apparently, he's all right now and wants to sort everything out. I didn't wait to hear more; I shut the door in his face, that's what I did.'

'Oh, Maureen, how upsetting.' Kate sipped her tea. 'How do you feel about Fenella's death?' She wondered if Maureen felt justice had been done by somebody? Had she been shocked? Relieved? Worried?

Another shrug. 'No idea. She's no great loss anyway.'

Kate had never seen anyone knit so fast or so furiously. Click, click, click. She hoped she wasn't pushing Maureen into places she didn't want to go. She had coped for years on pills that had suffocated her feelings, and Kate knew from experience where that could lead. Now, more than ever, she was determined to help Maureen if she could.

Maureen, who'd suddenly stopped knitting and spent a moment staring at the fire, looked up at Kate and asked, 'Do *you* think Kevin Barry killed Fenella?'

'It seems Kevin Barry had an alibi, drinking in The Tinners with Seymour, according to the police. And so Fenella's husband had an alibi too. Now where does that leave us?'

Maureen sniffed. 'You saw her first after she was killed. Do you think she suffered?'

Kate wondered from Maureen's fierce expression if she was hoping the answer would be yes. 'It's you that suffered most, Maureen. You need to get answers to a lot of questions, and not least from your husband. Do you know where he's been?'

'No, I don't know. I didn't ask.'

'Perhaps he just wanted to say he was sorry?'

'Well, he's ten years too late,' Maureen snapped.

'Yes, Maureen, it's been ten years, and now,' Kate said gently, 'perhaps you need to move on.'

'Move on? Where on earth would I move on to?' Maureen asked, blowing her nose.

'You're a young woman. You're what? Forty-two?'

'Forty-three.'

'Perhaps you should think about getting a job?'

'What would I do? I'm too old to start something new.'

'No, you're not, Maureen. Just for a start there's lots of seasonal jobs coming up, isn't there? How about working in a shop or a café or something?'

'I used to do a bit of cleaning sometimes,' Maureen said. 'That's all I'm good for.'

'Well, all the guesthouses and self-catering places in the Tinworthy villages must be screaming out for cleaners for the summer. It would be some extra cash.' She wanted to add, 'to pay for some heat'.

'Yeah, well.' Maureen patted Barney's head. 'Nice dog.'

'Yes, he's a lovely dog. Have you ever thought about getting one?'

Maureen snorted. 'I've got a cat so I don't need a ruddy dog. But you're determined to sort me out, aren't you?'

'Only because I think you're worth sorting out. And you need to get out of *here*.'

'That's what everyone says.'

'Perhaps everyone's right,' Kate said, getting to her feet. 'I'd best be home before it gets dark. Thanks for the tea.'

Maureen got up slowly, hesitated for a moment, then said, 'Would you like to see Lucy's room?'

'Yes, I'd like that very much.' Kate had a feeling about what she was likely to find as she followed Maureen up the stairs and into the pink-walled bedroom. She saw rose-patterned curtains, a duvet cover patterned with cute puppies, shelves full of soft toys and dolls, and a pair of small fluffy pink slippers.

'She liked pink,' Maureen said.

'She certainly did,' Kate agreed, feeling distinctly moist-eyed as she turned towards the door. It was the little pair of slippers that had got to her, the fur flattened where Lucy's feet had once rested. She gazed at the room for a moment, then turned to walk down the stairs where she attached the lead to Barney's collar and headed towards the front door.

'Promise me you'll get in touch with me anytime you need to,' Kate said, fishing in her bag and producing a card. 'Here's my address and phone numbers. Promise?'

'I promise,' Maureen said and – for the first time – Kate deciphered a trace of a smile on her face.

As she walked home, Kate thought about Maureen. She'd made a tiny bit of headway and it felt as if Maureen was beginning to trust her. It was a good feeling. But Kate couldn't really understand why the husband had come back on the scene after so many years. And she couldn't understand why Maureen wouldn't allow Kevin to show her the proof he claimed to have. There were still so many unanswered questions. And then Kate thought about the little pair of pink slippers and the bedroom, which was now a shrine. She decided she must try to think of something else because she was becoming obsessed with Maureen's problems.

Tomorrow she'd get her own bedroom painted.

7

The following morning Kate painted three walls of her bedroom while Angie rolled her sleeves up for once and prepared Sunday lunch. As she sat down to eat at around two o'clock, she decided the fourth wall could wait until the next day. It was the tricky one anyway, with fiddly parts, nooks, crannies and alcoves, and the bit around the window that wouldn't close properly.

After lunch she relaxed on the sofa in the kitchen and glanced at the Sunday papers. There was that headline again:

Still no arrest for Cornish village killer!

It went on to say that Detective Inspector Forrest had confirmed that their only suspect so far had been released from custody.

By five o'clock Kate decided she needed some fresh air; she needed to get away from the smell of paint, and the dog was begging for a walk.

'Fancy a stroll along the beach?' she suggested to Angie.

'It's getting late,' Angie protested. 'I'll just stay home and maybe have a little nightcap later.'

'Haven't you had enough today? You drank three-quarters of the bottle of Merlot at lunchtime,' Kate snapped, feeling irritated.

'I have a strong constitution,' Angie replied, looking back at the magazine she was reading.

'Well, I'm going to have a wander along the beach,' Kate said, donning her coat and pulling on her boots.

As she and Barney approached the shore she could see no one around except for some dedicated surfers still out at sea. As the clocks had just gone forward that day, the sun still had another hour before it dipped beneath the horizon, casting a mixture of copper and mauve as it sank. Kate wanted to sit somewhere quiet to fully take it in; it was so beautiful. She plonked herself on a rock and stared out at the Atlantic, relaxing as she listened to the sound of the waves crashing onto the beach. The tide was coming in and in another half hour or so the rock she was sitting on would be completely submerged. Then she noticed some of the surfers coming out of the water, and one wetsuit-clad figure was heading in her direction.

'Mrs Palmer, I believe?' said a man's voice with an American accent.

Kate found herself looking into a pair of warm brown eyes. 'Detective Inspector Forrest, I presume?' she replied.

'Correct!' he said. 'Except I get called Woody when I'm not on duty. And what brings you to the beach on this Sunday evening?'

'The dog needed a walk and I needed some fresh air,' she said. She wanted to add 'and I have an alcoholic sister who's driving me nuts' but didn't. He sat down on a rock a couple of feet away and laid his surfboard on the sand. The wetsuit showed his toned figure to advantage and she wanted to stare at him but couldn't. *Don't get smitten*, she told herself. *He's bound to be married and, even if he isn't, you are* not *looking for anyone else, Kate Palmer*!

'Do you enjoy surfing?' she asked. What a daft question! *Of course* he enjoyed surfing, otherwise why on earth would he be down here on a Sunday evening?

'I sure do. I'm a California boy, you know. Grew up on a surfboard but, hey, the water's a whole lot warmer over there than it is here! Do you surf, Mrs Palmer?'

'Kate.'

'OK, do you surf, Kate?'

'No,' Kate admitted, 'I've never tried it but then I'm not much of a swimmer.'

'Shame. It's the most exhilarating thing on earth. Well, *almost*.' She could see he was smiling at her and was relieved her blushes weren't visible beneath the darkening skies.

She couldn't resist asking, 'How's the murder inquiry coming along?'

He pulled a face. 'Slowly.'

Kate hesitated for a moment. Should she tell him about Maureen and Kevin rowing in the churchyard? It probably had nothing to do with Fenella's murder so she decided against mentioning it.

Woody Forrest stood up. 'Unfortunately, I can't discuss anything much about the case outside of the police station. But if you ever have any information at all that may be relevant, however trivial, then please come along and tell us.'

'I will,' she said.

'Good. And perhaps the next time I see you in The Gull you'll allow me to buy you a drink?'

'That would be lovely,' Kate said truthfully.

She sat on the rock for a good fifteen minutes after he left, watching the water coming closer and closer, and the sky becoming purple, deep in thought. She was becoming more and more fascinated by this murder case. Like everyone else she'd thought it *must* be this Kevin Barry who'd inexplicably returned after years in prison. But how could it be when he had an alibi? Obviously, the police weren't convinced, otherwise why would they have released him?

She walked along the shoreline slowly, deep in thought, when Barney's hysterical barking took her attention. The dog, tail wagging furiously, was about fifty yards ahead of her, standing in amongst the rocks at the foot of the cliff, over what appeared to be a heap of clothes or something washed up on the beach.

'Leave it alone, Barney, whatever it is!' she ordered as she walked towards the dog. It was awful the stuff people chucked into the sea, too lazy to go to the tip. She nearly walked past but something compelled her to take a closer look.

As she drew nearer she felt her heartbeat increasing; this wasn't just a bundle of clothes… she could see a shoe protruding from the pile. And there was obviously a foot inside it. She paused and took a breath, and then took a deeper breath, summoning up her courage. She walked towards what she was almost certain must be a body.

Another dozen steps confirmed her fear. It was the body of a man lying face down. Kate pushed away the hysterical dog and turned the body over as well as she could. He appeared to have drowned but there was a massive cut above his right ear. In spite of the awfulness of the situation, her training kicked in. As she automatically tried to resuscitate him she realised who he was. There was a long scar running all the way down his cheek.

The man was Kevin Barry.

8

Woody Forrest must have changed out of his wetsuit mighty quickly, Kate thought as she stood further back on the beach and watched him organise the spotlights being set up. Now he was ordering the men to tape off the area round the body. Fortunately, the tide was on the turn. She felt cold, shivery and a little sick. Thank God she'd had her mobile phone with her. The police had arrived very quickly; she guessed they must all be on high alert. Woody Forrest had asked her to wait, and now he was walking back towards her.

'How long after I left the beach would you say it was when you came across the body?' he asked her. 'I know you've had a dreadful shock but it helps if I can get your immediate reaction.'

'Probably about fifteen or twenty minutes,' she replied, her teeth chattering.

'And was there anyone else on the beach at that time?'

'No,' Kate said. 'It was deserted – it was almost dark. I was just about to go home when the dog started barking and that's what drew it – him – to my attention. He looked like he'd been in the water for a little while.'

'He must have been floating around while I was still surfing,' Woody said, pulling a face. 'Not a comfortable thought.'

'Could he have jumped off the cliff?' Kate asked. 'I noticed a nasty wound above his ear.'

'Yes,' Woody said. 'You're right to be concerned about the gash above the ear. My guess is that our friend was killed by a blow to the head before being dumped in the water. Look, I think you should go home; this has been an awful shock for you. Can I ask you to come to the police station first thing in the morning? Or no – perhaps it's better that I come to interview you at your home?'

'Whatever's easiest for you,' Kate said.

'Are you OK to walk home? Unfortunately, I've got to be here but I could send one of my constables with you.'

Kate took a deep breath. 'I'm fine, thanks. I'll be on my way in a minute.'

Kate collapsed gratefully onto the sofa at the far end of the kitchen,

Angie glanced at her. 'Don't tell me walking the dog is *that* strenuous!'

Kate took a deep breath. 'I've just found a body. A dead body. On the beach. Forgive me for feeling shell-shocked!'

Angie stopped pouring her drink, gin bottle in mid-air. '*What?*'

'You heard. I found a body – Kevin Barry's body. Just make me a strong coffee, will you, and laced with brandy?'

'You found *Kevin Barry's* body? Tell me you're kidding!'

'I'm not kidding. And he'd been murdered.'

'Oh my God!' Angie laid down the gin bottle and bent down to put her arms round Kate. '*Tell* me!'

Kate related the details of her discovery as Angie got up and then produced a large goblet of brandy. 'Drink this!' she ordered.

Angie came into her own on the rare occasion that she – the big sister – could look after Kate. Where alcohol was the medicine of choice, Angie was on safe ground. Nevertheless Kate was very grateful and felt the warmth flow back into her body after a couple of sips.

'Who would murder Kevin Barry?' Angie asked no one in particular.

'That,' Kate replied, 'is the million-dollar question.'

*

Kate found it impossible to get to sleep burdened with the image of Kevin Barry's body lying on the beach and the still-strong smell of paint in her bedroom. Then she recalled seeing the detective in that wetsuit with his nice firm body and his lovely brown eyes – such a sharp contrast to poor Kevin with that awful mark on the side of his head. What was even more terrifying was the fact that there must still be at least one murderer at large.

Then, desperate to divert her thoughts, she wondered what Woody's real name was. He was American; Californian. A beach boy! But he was almost certainly married. Although he had offered to buy her a drink so, perhaps, he wasn't.

In a further effort to obliterate the image of Kevin's body, she tried to think about other things. How unpredictable life can be! She reminded herself yet again that you should enjoy every moment and take no one or nothing for granted. Her thoughts wandered to Angie.

Kate desperately wanted to wean her sister off alcohol or at least persuade her to cut down. Because – from the time she got up in the morning until she fell into bed at night – Angie's mission in life was to dull her senses. Why? Was it genetic, as their mother had thought? Surely Kate had the same blood coursing around in her veins so how come she rarely felt depressed? Kate knew that her mother would have been relieved to know that she, Kate – the sensible younger sister – was here to look after her unfortunate sibling.

Then, as she continued to lie sleepless, she thought about her two sons. Tom, now a civil engineer up in Edinburgh, was married to Jane, who was expecting a baby boy in mid-August. Kate hoped that her first grandson might be born on her own birthday, which was the sixteenth.

And there was Jack, out there in Australia, so far away. From the time he was a boy and had seen some programme on television about the wide-open spaces, the sport and the lifestyle, he'd been determined to go there. He'd worked his way up in the building trade to become a project manager and, the moment he discovered that project managers were required in Australia, he was off like a bullet. Kate had cried her eyes out but she knew it was best for him; he'd have the life he wanted out there in Brisbane. Two years ago she'd flown out for a month's visit to find Jack loving his job, swimming in the sea every day and living with a beautiful girl called Eva.

Kate wanted to go back and once they'd paid off the central heating and the floorboards and got the window locking properly, she'd get saving again.

Alex, her ex-husband, had, of course, been out there a couple of times, the first time with his newish wife and the second time without her because she'd wisely absconded (no bad judge). Alex worked for an airline as an aircraft engineer and got cheap trips. Kate's cheap trips had ended with the divorce, but it had been worth it to be rid of him and his endless womanising.

That had begun in Singapore where they'd spent the first two years of their married life and where Tom was born. Kate had enjoyed Singapore; the luxury flat, the live-in help, the social life and the friendships formed. At least she'd made friends with her own sex, which was more than she could say for Alex. She hadn't liked the constant heat and humidity and swore then that she'd never complain about the British climate again. But she did, of course, and Singapore was now a dim memory.

Cornwall suited her fine. She'd go up to Edinburgh for a long weekend after the grandson was born and she'd save up for another trip to Australia. She could look forward to both trips and that was helping to take her mind off things.

The image of Kevin had faded very slightly.

She finally got to sleep at half past three.

Dr Ross rang at eight o'clock.

'You're not coming in today,' he said to Kate. 'Not after what you've been through. I don't imagine you got much sleep?'

'I think I dozed on and off for about three hours,' Kate admitted.

'Well, take it easy if you can today. I think Detective Inspector Forrest will want a statement from you, but otherwise I'd stay at home because there's press absolutely everywhere. I should lock the door and keep out of sight.'

'Thanks, Andrew. I will.'

Kate felt exhausted but knew she probably wouldn't even be able to catnap today; her mind refused to switch off. Instead, she sat down in front of the television in the hope of finding a programme that would take her mind off things. And found herself watching a repeat of *Morse*, which, of course, got her thinking about murders again. She'd have to take a sleeping pill tonight.

And now, more than ever, Angie was convinced there was a serial killer roaming free.

'I *told* you so,' she said, 'but nobody listened. Everyone had it in for poor Kevin, didn't they? Well, they were *wrong*. I'm going back to my studio, *with* the saucepan.'

Kate couldn't argue with any of that.

At ten o'clock there was a knock at the door and Kate looked out cautiously in case the press were around. She was relieved, and not a little pleased, to see Woody Forrest on the doorstep.

'I'm afraid I'm here in an official capacity,' he said ruefully as he came in.

'I rather suspected you might be,' Kate said, 'but that doesn't preclude you from having a coffee, does it?'

'Not at all,' he said, grinning.

She led him into the sitting room where he sat down next to the log burner.

'This is nice,' he said, looking around. 'And *warm*. It's so cold out there today and the police station's not much better.'

Kate headed off to make some coffee and reappeared shortly afterwards bearing a tray with a cafetière of coffee, mugs, milk and sugar.

'Just a drop of milk, please,' Woody said, tapping his waistline.

Kate handed him a mug, noting that he looked tired. Probably he'd not slept too well either.

'This will probably be my last case,' he said, suppressing a yawn. 'And it doesn't look like being an easy one.' He grinned at her. 'I'm getting far too old for all this malarkey.'

'Will you go back to the States?' *I hope not*, she thought.

He shook his head. 'Nope, I'm planning on staying here, for most of the time anyway. I've been living over here for so long now that I'm not sure I'd fit in back in the States now. Even if I do have to wear a wetsuit for surfing! But I digress, because now we must get down to the nitty-gritty, as you say over here.' He produced a file and a recorder from his briefcase. 'I'm going to take a statement from you, Kate, so just tell me – in your own words – your exact movements yesterday evening.' He switched on the recorder and said, 'I'm interviewing Mrs Kate Palmer, who found the body of Kevin Barry.' He gave the time and the date.

Kate did her best to recount her walk on the beach, omitting to mention Woody's wetsuited appearance, and how she'd followed the dog's frantic barking and found the body. She tried to be accurate as to the time but hadn't thought to consult her watch with the shock of her discovery.

He switched off the recorder for a moment. 'You *can* mention that you saw me on the beach,' he said with a smile. 'The time of death, I've been told, was at least twenty-four hours earlier.'

Kate gulped. 'But I saw him in Middle Tinworthy on Saturday afternoon,' she said.

'Really? Where did you see him?' he asked.

She told him about her walk round the churchyard and witnessing Maureen and Kevin at loggerheads. 'It didn't seem that important at the time,' she said, 'but it obviously is now.'

'It certainly is,' Woody said.

'Well, Kevin was desperately trying to persuade Maureen to listen to him, and there was something about a letter he'd written to her and some recording or other, but she was having none of it. He was telling her that he hadn't been driving the car that killed Lucy but she still seemed to blame him for being there at all.'

'Would you say that she was acting aggressively?' Woody asked.

Kate thought for a minute. 'Well, she picked up what looked like an urn or something and I truly thought she was going to brain him with it, but he moved away quickly.' Kate stopped and looked directly at Woody. 'But you don't think Maureen would…'

'I don't think anything. I just note the facts.' He began to place his file and recorder back into the briefcase.

'Yes, of course.'

He looked up and smiled. 'I'm hoping there isn't a Mr Palmer?'

'Not for years,' Kate said, smiling back. 'I moved here with my sister.'

'Well, there isn't a Mrs Forrest either so, perhaps, when all this is done and dusted, you might consent to come out to dinner with me?'

'I'll look forward to it,' Kate said.

Angie had been painting in the summerhouse during Woody's visit and was now crashing about in the kitchen, washing her hands.

'Couldn't you have persuaded him to stay a bit longer?' she asked grumpily as she watched Woody's silver BMW disappear down the driveway.

'No, I couldn't. He wasn't here on a social call.' Kate omitted to mention his invitation.

'Aren't you going to work today?'

'No, I've been given the day off. Unlike some people I didn't get my eight hours' sleep last night.'

Angie softened. 'It must have been horrible for you, Kate. God knows what I'd have done if I found a body like that – ugh! But what's scary is that there's either one person who's killed twice or there are two separate killers. Either way I'm not going over the doorstep today except to my studio!'

'Not even to the pub?'

'Oh, wait a minute, I've just remembered we've run out of gin!'

'Correction: *you've* run out of gin.'

'OK, OK, *I've* run out of gin! Maybe I'll have to switch to Scotch or something, but the trouble is I don't even *like* Scotch! Oh, shit! What am I going to do?'

'Well, bearing in mind that going teetotal doesn't appear to be an option, I'm going to finish painting my bedroom this morning so you can have the car if you want.'

'But do you think I can get to Lidl and back without being murdered?' Angie appeared to be genuinely worried.

'It's a possibility, I suppose,' Kate said drily. 'You'll just have to weigh up what's more important: the advantage of a bottle of Lidl's gin against you getting back alive.'

'It's a no-brainer,' Angie said after a moment. 'I'm off to Lidl. Where are the car keys?'

9

As she grabbed a sandwich at lunchtime, Kate was beginning to regret not going in to work. She'd painted the fourth wall of her bedroom, tricky bits and all, while feeling strangely happy. There was no *Mrs* Forrest! And Woody planned to ask her out! That did a lot to alleviate the horrors of the previous evening but left her feeling restless. She began to move her bedroom furniture around so that the head of the bed was directly under the window. She liked fresh air and this new arrangement gave her a lot more space in the rest of the room.

By mid-afternoon Kate decided that she and Barney needed their daily walk and some fresh air. This time she chose the coastal path, although it was a cloudy day and the views wouldn't be as spectacular as usual.

A few people, presumably tourists, were meandering along the beach, either unaware of last night's tragedy or else exploring the area in lurid fascination for that very reason. Kate herself felt a little weird as she strolled across the sand, past the rocks where she'd found Kevin's body, and along to the path that led up to Penhallion Cliff on the north side of the beach. The gulls wheeled overhead and the rollers crashed on the rocks beneath. It had begun to drizzle and, looking out to sea, she could see curtains of rain coming in from the horizon, which was rapidly obliterating the hazy outline of Lundy Island and the jagged coastline of Hartland Point to the north. To the south, the dramatic bays and inlets towards Trevose Head were already obscured by the falling rain.

Regardless of the weather, Kate thought, *we're so lucky to live here, murders or no murders.*

She'd walked quite some way – Barney running frantically hither and thither, sniffing the heather and the coarse grass that grew up here – when she spotted him again. Seymour Barker-Jones. This time he was sitting on a wooden bench, the one which had been erected in memory of Jonas Prendergast, a one-time local councillor, and which had been securely anchored onto a concrete base to prevent it from flying off to the Americas in the frequent gales.

Seymour was gazing out to sea, his dogs running around nearby.

As Kate approached, he looked up.

'Good afternoon,' Kate said politely.

'Good afternoon,' he said. 'I've been watching a container ship out on the horizon, but I can't see it now with the rain. I often wonder what they're carrying – probably cars, heading to Avonmouth.'

'Probably,' Kate agreed.

'I sat on this very seat with Fenella once,' he said, still staring out at the misty sea. 'Only once.' He turned around to look at her and she saw his eyes were full of tears. She wondered if she should sit down beside him, pat his hand, or what.

'It was a rare occurrence,' he continued, 'because she preferred to *ride* everywhere. She loved riding. Do you ride, Mrs Palmer?'

Kate sat down near, but not too near, him. 'No,' she replied. 'I've never really had the opportunity.' *Or the time, or the money, or the courage for that matter,* she thought.

'Pity,' he said. 'There's a wonderful riding school at Trebarrow, just a couple of miles along the coast.' He pointed vaguely north-wards. 'Thing is, Fenella's horse needs some exercising and there's no one to do it at the moment. The little mare's rather lively, so probably not suited to a novice.' He looked doubtfully at Kate.

'Probably not,' Kate agreed. Did he think she was about to take riding lessons? 'I think I'll stick to walking – not so far to fall!' For a brief moment she imagined herself on a galloping steed, toppling out of the saddle and hitting the ground at goodness-knows-how-many-miles-per-hour.

'Meg, Bella, *come*!' He stood up and called to the dogs. They came, wagging their tails and lay down obediently at his feet.

With that he raised his cap and headed off down another stony path, which Kate knew led to a small car park where he'd obviously left his Land Rover or whatever it was he drove, Meg and Bella still barking at his heels. Barney was set to follow them and she had to call him back and hang on to his collar until they'd disappeared.

Kate continued sitting and looking out to sea for a few minutes. She wondered if she was foolhardy wandering along the clifftops alone. She'd heard that most of the Tinworthy women were too terrified to open their doors or to leave their homes. There must surely be some personal local history involved in these tragedies, she reckoned, and so, hopefully, she wasn't on the killer's list, having only been here a few weeks. Nevertheless, she shivered and had a good look around as she stood up, before setting off back the way she'd come.

Kate found Angie, alive and well, unpacking four bottles of gin, having survived her trip to the supermarket.

Seeing Kate's face, Angie said, 'Well, it was *such* a good offer!'

Kate sighed. 'Obviously. Think I'll settle for a coffee though.'

'Enjoy your walk?'

'Yes, and I saw Seymour Barker-Jones again. He was sitting up there on that old wooden seat. He looked sad.'

Angie placed the bottles carefully into the cupboard. 'Well, he will be, I expect.'

'He's certainly not particularly chatty.' Kate sat down with her coffee. 'But, do you know what? I wouldn't know where to *begin* to solve this one. I mean, Kevin Barry was the main suspect, so where do they go from here? I suppose Kevin could have murdered Fenella before someone else murdered him. Then there's this old doctor, and the hotel owner's wife. And Seymour, I suppose. Not to mention Maureen Grey and her dodgy husband who's appeared out of the blue after ten years God-knows-where. And Kevin had a long-term girlfriend who he'd been staying with apparently. Perhaps they had a quarrel? Perhaps she was heartily sick of his carrying on with Fenella years ago and decided to kill them both?'

'Blimey, Kate, you've given this a lot of thought!' Angie said. 'But don't you forget my roaming serial killer. It doesn't have to be one of the locals, does it?'

'No, but I have a distinct feeling it is. And what I don't understand is why anyone would kill Kevin with a blow to the head and then chuck him into the sea.'

'To make sure any incriminating evidence is washed away, I expect,' Angie said. 'Like fingerprints. Anyway, it must be the easiest way to get rid of someone. Would look a bit weird if he or she started digging a grave, would it not?'

'Who knows? Like I said, I wouldn't know where to begin to solve this lot,' Kate said.

Sue was beside herself with excitement when Kate went back to work the following morning.

'Wow! You actually *found* the body on the beach! Beats picking up shells any day of the week! Rumour has it he wasn't only drowned but bludgeoned as well! Someone really didn't like him much, did they?'

'Someone certainly didn't,' Kate agreed.

'They're still awaiting the autopsy report, Dr Ross said,' Sue continued, 'but I think it's a foregone conclusion.'

Kate, looking round the crowded waiting room, didn't wait to hear about Sue's foregone conclusion and called in the first patient.

The eighty-year-old woman informed Kate that Billy Grey – Maureen's errant husband – was almost certainly the killer of both. Why else would he appear out of the woodwork after ten years? she asked. And he was keeping a very low profile, although he'd been seen around. He'd come back for a *purpose*. And it was the anniversary of the little girl's death. 'You mark my words,' she said.

The second patient wanted a blow-by-blow account of Kate's gruesome discovery on the beach. What had Kevin looked like? Were his eyes bulging? What was he wearing? Kate stared at the woman in disbelief; his sartorial taste formed the least of her memories.

Later in the morning she was informed that Jess Davey, Kevin's so-called (long-suffering) girlfriend, was a real bad lot. She'd put it about a bit too, said the young builder who'd been bitten by a stray dog he'd tried to befriend. Jess had had it in for Fenella for years, he said. *Well, why wait ten years?* Kate wondered. And surely she'd be unlikely to kill Kevin as well if she was so devoted to him?

In the course of her shift Kate was informed of at least six different characters who would have been more than happy to kill one, or both, and by the time she got home, she was more than ready to collapse into the armchair with one of Angie's high-strength gin and tonics.

'If you came in the kitchen door you probably wouldn't have looked at the phone,' Angie said as she appeared from the summerhouse. 'It's buzzing with messages.'

Kate had kicked off her shoes and, for a moment, wondered if she'd bother to check the landline. Probably somebody trying to sell her something, or telling her about some vast amount of money that she hadn't bothered to claim. Then she thought of Woody. Perhaps he'd left a message and so, wearily, she padded out to the hallway. Anyone she knew well would surely have contacted her on her mobile.

The female voice was high and hysterical.

'I'm in custody! I'm in bloody *custody*! And it's all thanks to you, Kate Palmer, my so-called *friend*! You told the police about me and Kevin arguing in the graveyard!' Here, Maureen's voice broke. 'They've been questioning me all day; they think I killed *both* of them! I don't even kill bloody flies! I open the window and push the damn things out! You said you'd help me and I trusted you. So help me now, for God's sake!'

Kate stood, rooted to the spot, rigid with shock. They'd arrested Maureen! *Maureen!* How could they? What evidence could they possibly have?

'You look like you've seen a ghost,' Angie muttered as she came down the stairs into the hall.

'Listen to this!' Kate said and played back the message, upping the volume.

'Oh my God!' Angie put her hand to her face. 'What on earth are you going to do?'

'Well, just for a start, I'm going to visit Maureen,' Kate said, looking at her watch. 'I'm sure she's allowed a visitor and I shall damn well insist.'

'Oh, Kate.' Angie put her arm round her sister. 'But you don't know for sure that Maureen didn't kill one or both of them, do you?'

'I'm certain she didn't do it. Call it a gut feeling, but I'm not usually wrong, Angie. I realise that now Kevin's out of the picture, she's going to be the most likely suspect. But I'm pretty sure that – unless they have something definite on her – they can't keep her in custody for more than twenty-four hours.'

'You watch too much crime stuff on TV,' Angie retorted.

'It's a good job that I do. Anyway, I'm going to change into jeans and a sweater and head up to the police station. Wish me luck!'

It was a forty-minute drive to the police station at Launceston and the first thing Kate noticed as she got out of the car was the group of reporters, mostly male, plus a camera crew, all looking bored.

A woman pushed herself forward, stamping out her cigarette as she did so. 'Are you here in connection with the murders?' she asked.

Kate wasn't prepared for this, so thought it best to say nothing.

'I'm here on a personal matter,' she muttered, heading towards the door.

'Are you Kate Palmer?' the female reporter asked, continuing to follow her.

How does she know my name? Kate was relieved to get inside.

The constable on duty looked about sixteen, complete with acne.

'I'd like to see Maureen Grey, please,' Kate asked.

The policeman glanced at her briefly. 'Visiting's not allowed,' he said, 'sorry.' He didn't sound in the slightest bit sorry.

'Well, is Detective Inspector Forrest on the premises? I'd like to speak to him.'

He looked at her for a little longer. 'Who's asking?'

'My name's Kate Palmer.'

'Just a minute.' He sighed as he picked up the phone. 'I've got a Kate Parker here wants to talk to you, boss.'

'Kate *Palmer*.'

'Kate *Palmer*,' he repeated, staring glassily at Kate. Then: 'Yessir,' and he replaced the phone. 'The detective inspector will see you shortly. Take a seat, please.'

Kate continued to stand and was about to study the noticeboard when Woody appeared.

'Ah, Mrs Palmer,' he said, smiling at her. 'Come with me, please.'

'I'm sorry to bother you,' Kate said, 'but I really want to see Maureen Grey. She left a message on my phone while I was at work and she was in great distress. Please!'

Woody opened the door to what was obviously his office and stood back to let her in.

'Take a seat,' he said.

Kate sat down in front of a desk strewn with paperwork and gazed at the wall, on which was tacked a huge map of all the Tinworthys – with various areas highlighted – and photographs alongside: Fenella, Seymour, Kevin, Maureen, and three others who she didn't recognise.

Woody sat down behind the desk and shuffled some papers to one side.

'She is here, isn't she?' Kate asked.

'Yes, she is. We've had to keep her here for the moment.' He looked directly at Kate. 'Five minutes,' he said. 'I can let you have five minutes.'

'Thank you,' Kate said. 'And, tell me, did you arrest Maureen purely on account of my telling you about her arguing with Kevin in the churchyard?'

'Not just that,' he said. 'We had several reasons to question her, not least the fact that she's now the person with the greatest motive to have killed both of them. She's not been arrested as such; she's helping us with our enquiries. I know you probably mean this kindly but—'

'Woody, *please*!' Kate interrupted.

He looked at his watch. 'Like I said, *five* minutes.'

'Thank you,' Kate said, standing up.

'And I'd like to speak to you afterwards,' he said as he led her along a short dark corridor, unlocked an unmarked door and ushered her into a room – or was it a cell? – about nine feet square, with a narrow window high up in the wall and a bed in the corner.

On the floor rested an empty plastic cup with what looked like the dregs of some tea in the bottom. Sitting on the bed, looking tear-stained and tired, was Maureen in a black jumper and grey slacks.

'Oh, Maureen!' Kate said, sitting down beside her as Woody disappeared back into the corridor, locking the door again behind him. 'I'm truly sorry if what I told them has resulted in your being in here. But surely that's not enough to keep you in for long?'

Maureen sniffed and fumbled up her sleeve, withdrawing a tissue. After a hearty blow she said, 'It didn't bloody well help – that and the letter.'

'What letter?'

'The letter Kevin Barry wrote to me while he was in jail, saying it was Fenella who'd been driving when Lucy was killed.'

'But surely that doesn't prove anything?' Kate asked.

'Well, if I believed him, I suppose it might have made me want to kill Fenella. I might have wanted to kill them *both*, come to think of it! But I couldn't kill *anybody*, and they have to believe that.'

'I believe you, Maureen,' Kate said.

'You do?'

'Yes, I do. I'm a pretty good judge of character. Anyway, how on earth would *you* have managed to bash Kevin on the head and then chuck him in the sea?'

Maureen sat up straight and stared at Kate. 'Is that what happened? They wouldn't tell me anything other than that his body was found on the beach.'

'*I* found it,' Kate said.

'Oh my God! What a nightmare! You've really got yourself involved in all this one way or the other, haven't you?'

Kate grimaced. 'You're right, I have. But I'll tell you what, Maureen, I'm going to see it through. I'm going to prove your innocence by finding out who *did* kill Fenella and Kevin.'

'How do you plan to do that?'

'I don't know yet, but I'll find a way.' She hoped she sounded more confident than she felt.

Just at that moment the door was unlocked and the young constable said, 'Time's up, Mrs Parker!'

Kate gave Maureen a tight hug. 'It doesn't fill you with confidence when they can't get your name right! But don't worry, Maureen, it'll all be OK.'

She headed towards the door. '*Palmer*,' she said to the constable, 'not Parker.'

As he led her back along the corridor, Woody appeared. 'Can I have that word, please?'

'Yes, of course.' Kate followed him into his office and sat down opposite him again.

'How did it go, Kate?' he asked from behind the desk.

'Well, five minutes isn't very long,' Kate replied. 'But I'm more sure than ever that she's not involved with these murders. Apart from anything else, how could a slim person like her possibly clobber a man and then chuck him into the sea?'

Woody regarded her steadily. 'No,' he agreed, 'she probably couldn't *on her own*, but she may have helped, aided and abetted.'

'What do you mean?' Kate was genuinely astonished.

'What I mean is that her husband could have done it. Did you know he'd come back on the scene?'

'Yes, she told me. But she didn't want to know and she shut the door in his face.'

'That's not strictly true,' Woody said, 'because he's been seen going into and coming out of the house, according to the neighbours anyway. But he's never there when we go looking for him of course.'

'So where is he now?'

Woody sighed. 'You tell me. His mother says he's not with her. They're looking for him as we speak, but your friend Maureen's giving nothing away.'

'Perhaps she's still loyal to him despite everything that's happened,' Kate said.

'Could be misplaced loyalty. And just one more thing. When you found Kevin Barry washed up on the beach, did you remove his mobile phone by any chance?'

'His *mobile phone*?' Kate stared back at him. 'Why would I do that? I didn't touch him apart from turning him over.'

'And you don't remember seeing a mobile phone anywhere around?' Woody persisted.

'No, of course not! Not that I was looking for one.'

Woody smiled. 'It was just a thought, something Maureen said. Apparently, he was thrilled with the phone Jess gave him and carried it with him everywhere, twenty-four/seven, so it seems strange that it wasn't in any of his pockets. We may, of course, find it where he was staying.'

'What's so important about a mobile phone?'

'Only what Maureen's told us – that he recorded a conversation he had with Fenella, which proves *she* was driving.'

'So how long will you keep Maureen here?'

'No longer than we have to,' he replied, 'but we'll be keeping a close surveillance on the house. In the meantime I'd ask that you keep your distance from the Greys.'

Kate was still shocked that Maureen's husband had been seen going into the house when Maureen had been so dismissive of him. *Could* they have killed Kevin together? And Fenella too? As a couple surely they had every reason to hate both Fenella and Kevin – but enough to kill them both?

'To change the subject,' Woody said, smiling, 'how do you fancy a meal out tomorrow night? And well away from here? And' – he looked serious all of a sudden – 'no talking shop of course. Officially I shouldn't be socialising with any witnesses.'

All thoughts of Maureen were suddenly washed away. 'That's a lovely idea!'

'So, how about I pick you up around seven?'

'That's fine. I'll be ready.'

10

As she drove home Kate's mind was in turmoil, not least because of her forthcoming date with Woody and what Angie might have to say about it. But, more than anything, she wondered if she'd misjudged Maureen. Could she possibly be the killer? Then, almost immediately, she thought, *No, I'm still sure she's innocent.*

When she got home she saw Angie painting away in her 'studio', so she sat down beside the log burner with a mug of coffee.

And she renewed her promise to herself that she'd do her best to try to solve this thing because she needed to prove Maureen's innocence. She felt responsible for the suspicion falling on Maureen because of what she'd told Woody. Was she capable of solving a crime like this? But, she thought, as a nurse she always had to follow clues from patients' symptoms to diagnose and solve problems. She was good at extracting information from people because she was naturally interested and curious, she had an analytical brain and she could more easily integrate and ask questions than a detective might be able to. And surely all these years glued to Agatha Christie, *Morse*, *Midsomer Murders* and the rest stood her in good stead! She felt sure she must have picked up some ideas.

She'd make a list of all the possible suspects and, by hook or by crook, she'd get to know them all. And, with a bit of luck, she might get a few pointers from Woody if she could only extort some information from him.

There was still no sign of Angie, who was plainly engrossed in her latest masterpiece. Kate only needed a sheet of paper on which to make her list. She grabbed a notebook from the desk drawer in the hallway and then sat down by the log burner again, pen poised.

She had to list Maureen, if only because her husband seemed to be such an elusive character, and she couldn't remember his name. Did she call him Mr Grey, M's husband, or what? She wrote, *the Greys*; it was indeed a grey area. Each of them had every reason to hate both Fenella and Kevin if there was some doubt as to who was driving on that fateful day. And neither Maureen nor the husband had been at the WI meeting. Furthermore, their house was a mere ten-minute walk away from the village hall.

Next was the pair from The Atlantic Hotel – Ed and Sandra Miller – neither of whom she'd yet met. That would have to be rectified somehow or other. They might never come to the surgery but at least she could access their records so she might find some excuse to contact them. Kate felt it was unlikely Mr Miller was a suspect but – from what she'd heard – Sandra Miller was a hot-tempered, passionate sort of woman who certainly had a motive for killing Fenella, if not Kevin. And she *had* been outside at the time of Fenella's murder.

The retired doctor, Dickie Payne, with the disabled wife was another matter. She could almost certainly exclude the wife, assuming that she was as frail as everyone said she was. She might have reason to visit this lady, but what about her husband? And, being a doctor, he was unlikely to visit the surgery for any minor ailment he could diagnose himself. Kate left a space on the sheet of paper for any ideas she might have there.

Seymour, of course, could not be excluded. Yes, it was common knowledge that his wife was having it off with every Tom, Dick and Harry, but everyone agreed that he'd been aware of that for years. Why – after leading such separate lives for so long – would he become sufficiently incensed to kill her? Seymour was a man of considerable status. She'd heard from several sources that he had an important job with the government; one or two even suggested that he was connected with MI5. What would suddenly make him risk all that? She couldn't rule him out, but mainly because she couldn't rule anybody out.

Who else? Kate chewed her pen for a moment. Then she remembered Kevin's so-called girlfriend, Jess Davey. Had she been so very jealous of Fenella? And, if she had, why would she have waited ten years for Kevin to reappear before she murdered her one-time rival? And did she kill Kevin as well? Like the Greys, it could have been a joint effort as far as Fenella was concerned, but *Kevin*?

And Kevin could, Kate supposed, have murdered Fenella, although he had an alibi, but she'd have to look into that. It came back to the question: was there one killer, or two?

Kate hadn't heard Angie coming in as she was so engrossed in her list.

'What on earth are you scribbling there?' Angie asked, kicking off her shoes.

'Just toying with a list of possible suspects for these murders,' Kate replied.

'Why would you do that?'

'Because it intrigues me.' Kate decided Angie didn't need to know that she was going to do her damnedest to find the culprit or culprits.

'I should let the lovely detective deal with all that,' Angie said. 'I'd even put aside my paints for a day or two to help him.'

Kate took a deep breath. 'There's something I have to tell you.'

'Oh yeah?' Angie was padding her way back into the kitchen. 'Have you seen that half-full bottle of gin I left in here by any chance?'

'No, I haven't. It'll be where you left it. But I've got something—'

'I could swear I left it on the work surface next to the fridge,' Angie interrupted.

'Well, I haven't touched it.' Kate sighed as she folded up her sheet of paper carefully. She was going to have to work out how to meet and suss out all these characters on her list in the vague hope she might impress Woody with some of her observations.

'Angie, there's something I have to tell you,' she said yet again as Angie reappeared clutching the gin bottle with one hand and a glass full of ice in the other.

'Have we any lemons?'

'Shut up for a moment! The lemons are in the fridge where they always are. I have something to tell you.'

'What's that then?' Angie called out as she headed back into the kitchen in search of lemons.

'The lovely detective is taking me out to dinner tomorrow night.'

Angie came back into the room and set down her glass – filled to the top, slice of lemon in position, ice tinkling – on the coffee table.

There was silence for a moment. Then Angie asked pointedly, 'How did you manage *that*?'

'I didn't *manage* anything,' Kate retorted. 'I went to see Maureen Grey, who's temporarily in custody at the police station, and chatted with Woody afterwards. And he asked me out. And I'm going.'

'I bet you are,' Angie said, taking a large gulp. 'Well, full marks to you. I don't suppose you mentioned that you had a lovely, lonely, needy older sister?'

'Strangely enough I didn't. But he has seen you several times so perhaps your loveliness and neediness failed to impress him.'

'I must be losing my touch then,' Angie said sadly, taking another large gulp. 'Well, when he gets bored with you and your silly list, do tell him I'm here to offer light relief. Anyway, he's not supposed to hobnob with witnesses, is he?'

'Probably not,' Kate replied. 'So don't go telling anyone.'

'Just don't go falling for him or something.' Angie took a large gulp of gin.

Why shouldn't I? Kate wondered. But she said nothing.

Kate didn't know where Woody was likely to be taking her but decided casual was probably best. She selected her one and only cashmere sweater, which was black, and teamed it with an emerald-green pencil skirt and long black leather boots. She paid special attention to her make-up and hair and she polished the boots. She felt sure that all policemen would treat their footwear to a daily spit and polish, a bit like the army. Then she wondered if Woody had been a policeman in the States before he came to the UK. And why had he come over here? There was so much to find out about this attractive man.

Angie had taken the car and gone to the cinema in Wadebridge. Kate wasn't sure how much she really wanted to see the film as opposed to how much she *didn't* want to see Kate going out with Woody. Kate was a little worried about her sister; was she really so lonely and needy? She'd have a heart-to-heart with her at a suitable time. The trouble with Angie was that she had too little to do other than daub paint onto canvas all day long, which gave her far too much time to daydream, mostly about men. Because, for sure, Angie still hoped to meet someone. She'd never given up looking for Mr Right. Even her late husband – who'd adored her and put up with no end of her drunken binges – had only been Mr *All*-Right, according to Angie. They'd jogged along for years before Angie thought she'd finally met Mr *Completely*-Right in the form of a 'double-glazing and conservatory specialist'. He turned out to be Mr *Definitely*-Not-Right and she'd been extremely lucky that George, her long-suffering husband, had taken her back. And now here she was, at nearly sixty years of age, still hoping to be swept off her size-seven feet.

*

Woody arrived, looking immaculate in a crisp white shirt under a pale blue cashmere sweater and dark trousers, at precisely two minutes after seven. His silver BMW appeared to have been polished up for the occasion, and he'd obviously gone to some length to present himself and his car in the best possible light.

'As I told you we need to get right away from Tinworthy,' he said. 'I could do without bumping into anyone from round here.'

'That's fine by me,' Kate said as she got into the passenger seat and noted that he'd had the inside of the car valeted as well. Was he always so neat and tidy or was this purely for her benefit?

As they drove off he asked, 'I've booked The Edge of the Moor. Do you know it?'

'No,' Kate replied, 'but I've heard it mentioned, and the comments always seem to be favourable.'

'Good,' he said. 'It's one of the few places where I can guarantee getting a great steak.' He glanced at her sideways. 'And now you're going to tell me you're vegetarian!'

Kate laughed. 'No, I'm not, although I must admit I eat a lot less red meat these days. But I do love my Sunday roast.' She'd starved herself since breakfast-time and hoped he couldn't hear her tummy rumbling. 'I think I might just manage a steak as well,' she added. *Understatement of the year*, she thought, *I could eat the whole animal right now.*

They chatted about the Cornish weather, the lack of trains to their part of the North Cornish coast and the fact that it took an hour to get to some decent shops. And they both agreed that they wouldn't want to live anywhere else.

'Where *do* you live, Woody?' Kate asked.

'Lower Tinworthy, of course!' he said. 'Right opposite you, on the slope up towards Penhallion. You probably pass my place every time you walk the dog.'

'Really?' Kate was astounded. She'd seen several houses and cottages across the little valley but never dreamed he lived in one of them. She'd better not tell Angie, who was quite liable to get out her binoculars to study all the windows.

'I bought it five years ago,' he said, 'when I came to live down here. I used to come to surf, you know, and then I saw this cottage up for sale and I thought, *hey, why not?* I'd been with the Met up in London for over thirty years and figured it was time for a change. There was a vacancy for a detective inspector in this area, and here I am. I think they were glad to put me out to grass.'

'And you've no regrets?'

'None at all. Mind you, I did think that coming here would be a nice sleepy prelude to retirement but nobody told me that the locals would be stabbing each other with bread knives or drowning each other. Perhaps I should have gone to the Outer Hebrides or somewhere, but I wasn't too sure how good the surf would be up there.'

Kate laughed. 'They saw you coming!'

'They sure did! But tonight we're not going to discuss who might have killed whom, or anything else to do with what's been going on. You OK with that?'

'Yes, I'm OK with that,' Kate said, although she'd really have liked to discuss her list with him. But what was a hobby for her was his everyday job and she respected his desire to get away from that.

It was becoming dark now as they headed up and away from Higher Tinworthy, the road meandering through rocky outcrops, with occasional sheep grazing by the roadside, towards Bodmin Moor. They drove in silence for a few minutes before he turned into the car park of an ancient, rustic, rambling one-storey building.

'This looks like the sort of place where smugglers might arrive any minute,' Kate observed, 'or even Poldark!'

'Well, apparently it does have a history of smuggling, a bit like Jamaica Inn,' Woody said. 'I guess you've been to Jamaica Inn?'

'Oh, I have,' Kate said as she got out of the car. 'It was exploring all the locations of Daphne du Maurier's books that got me wanting to live in Cornwall in the first place.'

'She didn't get round to writing about The Edge though,' Woody said, 'but I reckon it's her kind of place.'

He shepherded her into the warmth of a long, low-ceilinged candlelit restaurant, with a bar in the middle and an open fire at both ends. They were shown to a well-polished oak table for two, with sparkling glass and silverware and a tiny tubular vase containing one real white rose.

'Lovely!' Kate looked round at the rough stone walls and the oak beams overhead. The restaurant was three-quarters full and the only sound that could be heard above the low buzz of conversation was some Spanish guitar music; possibly John Williams. Beautiful, and quite unexpected.

She liked everything on the menu but settled for a seafood starter and a fillet steak. She declined a cocktail and settled for a large glass of Malbec, while Woody contented himself with a small beer because he was driving.

'What a great place!' Kate enthused again, once their starters had been delivered to the table, wondering how many other ladies Woody might have brought here.

'I bet you're wondering if I bring lots of dates here,' Woody said with a wicked grin.

'Of course not!' Kate lied.

'Only a couple,' he went on, 'and one of them was my sister who'd come over on vacation.'

Kate wasn't about to ask who the other was. She liked his brown eyes and lustrous lashes. How come it was the guys who got the long lashes? No justice in the world. She liked the way his eyes crinkled at the corners too.

'And the other was my younger daughter,' he continued, 'who'd come down from London for a weekend. Talking of which, I'm going up to London to spend Easter Sunday with her, if I can manage to take one day off. Like I said before, I rarely bump into anyone from the Tinworthys up here, although I did see Fenella Barker-Jones with Dickie Payne on one occasion.'

'You *did?*' Kate was fascinated by the fact that they'd actually appeared in public together, having imagined Dr Dickie Payne scuttling in and out of Pendorian Manor under cover of darkness.

'Oh yes, they went lots of places together, well away from home. I think she ended up costing him a lot of money.'

So, Kate thought, *perhaps that was why he tried to end the relationship. Maybe she was bleeding him dry financially as well as physically.*

'Tell me about yourself, Kate,' Woody said, cutting into her thoughts at the same time as cutting into his steak, which was so rare it was practically running around the plate.

'Oh, I'm not very interesting,' she said as she sliced into her own medium-rare filet.

'Of course you are! Tell me!'

Kate told him about growing up in a small village in rural Berkshire, about nursing at St Thomas's Hospital in London, about marrying Alex Palmer and then going out to Singapore for two years. 'That was when I realised he was a serial philanderer,' she said. 'But Tom, my older son, was born out there and, when we got back to the UK, Alex swore to me that he'd changed. No more women, no more lies. I was pregnant with Jack when I realised that, not only was he being unfaithful, but he was still seeing the same woman he'd been having an affair with in Singapore. She'd come back as well.'

'You've had it really tough,' Woody said gently.

'It was. He ended up marrying this woman, but that didn't last long. You know what they say: when you marry your mistress you create a vacancy. Anyway, he bought us a house in West London, near Isleworth, appeared briefly on high days and holidays to say hello to the boys, and paid as little as he could get away with for their upkeep. As soon as I could get them into school and childcare I went back to full-time nursing at the local health centre.'

'And you're *still* working?'

'Well, I had ideas about retiring when we came down here but, by the time we got the house more or less the way we wanted it, I realised I'd still have to work, part-time though. But I enjoy it and it's a great way to meet the locals, because they're usually pleased to see me! What about you, Woody?'

'Me? Well, I was born and raised in Santa Monica. My dad was English, my mom was Italian.'

Ah, she thought, *hence the olive skin and these lovely brown eyes.*

'I was the youngest of three,' he went on, 'and from the time I was a little kid, I was fascinated by the law. I watched all the detective stuff on TV and the movies, did well at college and won this amazing prize – to study criminology at Oxford University in *England*. My dad was over the moon, particularly as he had a sister living about five miles out of Oxford.'

'*Oxford!*' Kate lay down her knife and fork. 'My goodness, you must have been bright!'

He smiled modestly. 'I guess I was just lucky and there wasn't too much competition around that year. Well, I got myself a degree, I got myself an English wife and then I got myself a job with the Metropolitan Police in London. We lived in Kent, had two girls and then, damnit, around fifteen years ago, Liz was diagnosed with breast cancer. She got the full treatment, we thought it was under control and that she was in remission or whatever. But then we discovered that it had spread all over the place and she died on the very day of our twenty-fifth wedding anniversary.'

'Oh, Woody.' Kate instinctively placed her hand over his, which was resting on the table. 'I'm so sorry.'

He turned his hand and squeezed hers. 'At least the girls were grown-up and independent. Carol was married and living up in Yorkshire; still is for that matter. And Donna's a drama teacher, recently broken up with her partner and now doesn't ever plan on wedded bliss or motherhood, she says. Values her independence too much.'

'And how about you?'

'Well, I got as far as I could go with the Met. The only promotions were going to Brits, and younger ones at that. So as I said, I'd been coming down to Cornwall to surf for several years, heard they needed a DI for the CID in this area, saw the cottage in Lower Tinworthy, and here I am!'

'You don't ever hanker to go back to California?'

'Not really. I left when I was young and my life is over here now. But I love going back on holiday. Dad died some years back, but I like to see my sister and brother, and Mom, who, would you believe, is ninety-one and still makes her own pasta every day!' He paused for a moment. 'Now, that's enough about me. Would you like a dessert?'

Kate patted her tummy. 'I couldn't eat another thing!'

'You like it here?' he asked anxiously.

'I love it here,' she replied truthfully.

'Then we'll come again,' he said, still holding her hand.

He'd been the perfect gentleman, driven her home, refused her offer of coffee because he was on duty early the following morning and suggested that they might go out somewhere else in the coming weeks. 'But I can't promise when because there's so much going on right now,' he said, then sighed and pinched the bridge of his nose. 'We've had to release Maureen Grey due to lack of evidence. She's got to remain at home and we'll be questioning her again as and when it's necessary, but there are no definite leads yet. When that happens, or someone else gets murdered – God forbid! – then I'm not going to be able to go anywhere. And for the moment I don't want to run the risk of us being seen together. You OK with that, Kate?'

'I'm OK with that,' Kate replied as he gave her a clandestine kiss on the cheek. It was the first time he'd referred to his work; she was pleased they'd talked about so many other things. And she sincerely hoped they would be able to go out together openly once this case was solved.

Because she was not a little smitten.

11

The following day her first patient was Mrs Ida Tilley, the cook-cum-housekeeper at Pendorian Manor. Kate had heard from several sources that she ruled the house with a rod of iron.

'It's me finger,' said Mrs Tilley, unwinding a pristine bandage from the length of her forefinger to reveal a row of neat stitches. 'They has to come out.'

'When did you do this?' Kate asked.

'The night the mistress died!' exclaimed Mrs Tilley. 'Ten days ago. Yes, ten days ago now.'

'How did you do it? It looks like a nasty cut.'

'I'm havin' to chop up vegetables for the next day's soup, and then I hear them police bangin' on the door. Bangin' away they are. And I hear Mr Seymour answerin' it, and then there's this kerfuffle and I'm hearin' the poor man cry out. Cried out, he did. Cried out like a banshee. Like a banshee, whatever that is.'

'But what about this cut, Mrs Tilley? How did you do it?'

'That's when I *did* it, of course! It was such a terrible sound, pierce your very heart, it would, and it made me slip with the knife, and that's somethin' I never does.' She looked at Kate as if she was simple. 'That's how I did it! I sliced right down me finger, I did, instead of the bleedin' onion. Now I comes to think of it, it was a bleedin' onion cos there was blood all over it. My finger was pourin' blood it was, pourin'. It was everywhere! *Everywhere!* But I'm not one to make a fuss, nurse, I never does. I don't go worryin' about myself cos I'm dedicated to that family, you know. *Dedicated*, I am.

And poor Mr Seymour! I've never seen a man so distressed, never. So I just sort of wrapped me finger up as best as I could and took a couple of paracetamols cos it weren't half sore.'

'I'm sure it was,' Kate said, snipping away.

'Got it stitched the next mornin', I did. Poor Mistress Fenella – what a tragedy! And poor Mr Seymour, he ain't been the same since.'

'Has he gone back to London yet?' Kate asked.

'Oh no, Mr Seymour's still at home, he is. Still at home, he is. Don't know why they won't let him go back. It's them police again. Them police. Why do they want him stayin' here – tell me that?'

'I really don't know, Mrs Tilley. But I suppose the police will want all the suspects to stay in the area until an arrest has been made.'

'*Suspect!*' Mrs Tilley exploded. 'He ain't no *suspect*! He were only out for an hour or so and everyone in The Tinners seen him, so how can he be a *suspect*?'

'Well, perhaps they want him to be here when they finally arrest someone,' Kate soothed.

'He's not even allowed to *bury* her, he ain't. Got to wait. That poor woman's stuck in a drawer somewhere! A *drawer*! That's where they put them, isn't it? In a drawer in a fridge? I've seen it on the telly. Poor Mistress Fenella! She didn't like the cold.' She paused for breath. 'Have you done?'

'Yes, I have but I've only taken out every other stitch because it's jagged and hasn't knitted as well as I'd like. If you come back to me in another week I'll take the rest out then. Just be careful next time you're chopping vegetables.'

'Well, I don't normally have people screaming like banshees when I'm chopping me onions, and let me tell you I've been chopping vegetables for forty years without as much as a scratch. *Forty* years! And that knife was *sharp*! But poor Mistress Fenella had a sharper one go *right through her*! And to think she was probably only using it to cut that lovely cake I made. She always asked me to make them cakes for the Women's Institute. She won prizes for them you know. *Prizes*.' Mrs Tilley contemplated this for a moment. 'What was it called? The night of the long knives? Was that a film now? I didn't see it if it was.' She didn't seem to require an answer. 'Well, I'd best be goin'. I've better things to do that hang about round here.'

And off she went.

As Kate updated Mrs Tilley's notes she mulled over the new information she'd been given. From the little she knew of Seymour Barker-Jones he didn't seem like the kind of man who'd lose control, never mind scream like a banshee. Was he genuinely distraught or was he just a good actor?

Kate's next chance to get to know another of the suspects on her list came on the following Monday morning when she reported for duty.

'Kate, would you be prepared to pay a visit to the Paynes, in Higher Tee?' the receptionist asked as Kate checked in. 'Mrs Payne is the wife of the old senior partner who's retired now. She's quite frail and needs a dressing changed on her leg ulcer. Dr Payne's her main carer and looks after her well, but he's never keen on doing the dressings.'

'Of course,' Kate said, glancing at her schedule for the day. 'Looks like I've got a fairly quiet period between eleven and twelve.'

The Paynes lived in a large detached Victorian house in Higher Tinworthy, not far from Pendorian Manor, the home of the Barker-Joneses. Kate had only been up here a couple of times before and had been impressed by the area and the views.

The Paynes' front door was painted pillar-box red. As Kate rang the bell she looked at the pristine front garden where the dying daffodils, with their withering leaves, had been pleated and folded into need little pyramids.

The door was opened by a tall, very thin man, slightly stooped and with a shock of white hair. He wore a checked shirt and a tie with some crest or other on it, a grey V-necked pullover, and grey trousers with a tweed sports jacket. The ensemble was offset with some tartan 'old-man type' slippers. He was the epitome of respectable British elderly middle-class manhood in the 1950s.

'Ah, good morning, nurse! I'm Richard Payne,' he said brightly and it was then that Kate noticed his appealing – if steely – blue eyes and winning smile. He looked like he'd been an attractive man; still was, for that matter.

He led her into the hallway and then into a very large, well-proportioned sitting room. The interior of the house was exactly as Kate expected it to be, with well-polished parquet flooring, mahogany furniture and heavily swagged curtains. There was an absence of rugs on the floor except for the one in front of the fireplace, presumably to clear the way for the wheelchair-bound Mrs Payne.

Kate knew from the files that Mrs Payne suffered from multiple sclerosis, asthma and a variety of other complaints, and so expected to see a washed-out, frail little lady. But when she propelled herself into the room, Mrs Payne turned out to be an attractive woman with nicely coiffured iron-grey hair, smartly dressed in a pink jumper and navy trousers.

'This is my wife,' Dr Payne said unnecessarily.

She shook hands with Kate before saying, 'Go and make some coffee, Dickie, while I get to know our new friend here.' Then, as the doctor walked out of the room, she asked, 'What's your name?'

'I'm Kate – Kate Palmer.'

'Well, I'm Clare Payne and I'm pleased to meet you, Kate. Thank you for coming. I know how busy you must be, but it's so much easier for me to have home visits.'

'It's no problem,' said Kate, 'and I enjoy getting out and about. Now, let's have a look at this leg of yours.'

As Kate busied herself with dressings, she was aware of being scrutinised by Clare Payne.

'So, you're new here?' she asked.

'Yes,' Kate replied, 'I've been here about two months.'

'Still finding your way around?' asked the doctor as he reappeared with a tray of coffee, which he set down on the table. 'How do you like your coffee – and the Tinworthys?'

'I like my coffee with just a dash of milk and no sugar, please. And my sister and I have bought a cottage in Lower Tinworthy,' Kate replied, 'so I'm not too familiar with this area up here. But we both like it there very much.'

'Just so long as you don't get murdered,' Clare Payne said with feeling, glaring at her husband.

'Oh come *on*, Clare!' Dr Payne's hands shook as he was handing round the cups. Fortunately, there were saucers because the coffee had slopped everywhere. Did he have a medical problem or was he nervous? *Now why would he be nervous*? Kate wondered.

'Did you know Mrs Barker-Jones very well?' Kate asked.

'We'd been neighbours for ten years but we weren't what you'd call friends,' Clare replied.

Hmm, thought Kate, *that's not what I've heard*. She continued dealing with Clare's dressing.

'I was in the village hall the night of the murder and was called to inspect Fenella's body,' Kate said. 'It's not an evening I'm ever likely to forget.'

'I was told it was you who discovered the body of Kevin Barry on the beach,' the doctor said.

'Yes, it was,' Kate replied. 'I've not been sleeping well since, as you can imagine.'

'How awful for you,' said the doctor. 'How do you feel about wandering around in the evenings?'

'I don't go out much in the evenings,' she said.

'And do you lock your doors?' There was an inflection in his voice that made Kate shiver. He sounded almost amused. Kate was aware that he was studying her intently. Was her imagination running away with her or was there a strange look in his eyes?

'Oh, the door is usually locked anyway, but this business certainly doesn't stop me going out,' Kate said, sipping her coffee. 'My sister is convinced there's a serial killer on the loose, but I don't agree.'

'Neither do I,' said Clare.

There was silence for a moment. Then the doctor asked, 'Why do you not think there's a serial killer on the loose?'

'Because I think it's someone local,' Kate said, meeting his unblinking eye. 'I think he or she probably had a score to settle.'

'I think you're quite right,' said Clare. 'People seem to think that because I'm in this chair I don't know what's going on, but I do. And, of course, they suspect poor Dickie because he made that trip to the supermarket at the time Fenella was murdered. We'd run out of milk, you see. And here I was, all on my own, and I could hear the police sirens blaring away. I was quite terrified, and very relieved when Dickie got back. He'd had to go all the way to Camelford to get the milk.'

Kate couldn't think of what to say to this and neither, apparently, could Dickie. She concentrated on what she was doing, the Paynes concentrated on their coffees and nobody said anything. Clare Payne was supposed to be fragile, rumour had it, shielded from what was going on, unaware of her husband's philandering. In Kate's opinion Clare knew only too well what was going on, and probably knew about Dickie as well. Her body might be frail but her mind was sharp as a needle. Kate cast an eye at the doctor, who was staring out the window.

'I have some work to do in my study,' he said eventually. 'Will you excuse me?' Without waiting for an answer he headed out the door, still holding his coffee cup.

Now, thought Kate, *if I was watching this little scenario on the television, I would reckon he was as guilty as hell. He showed no sympathy at all for Fenella or Kevin. He said nothing about his trip to the supermarket. He was a cold fish. He could well be a suspect.*

But, try as she might, Kate couldn't imagine this tall, stooped Englishman shedding his tweed jacket and grey V-neck to wrench a knife from Fenella and then plunge it into her heart. Though at least he'd have known exactly where her heart was, which was more than could be said for most people.

'There now, almost finished,' Kate said into the silence as she finished bandaging. 'How does that feel, Mrs Payne?'

'It feels fine, and please call me Clare.'

'I will, Clare.'

'And please forgive Dickie for shooting off like that but he's got a lot on his mind at the moment.'

Has he now? Kate wondered.

'He was fond of Fenella, you know. Took it very badly, her murder.'

'I expect he did,' Kate murmured, thinking that 'fond' might be something of an understatement. How much did this woman know precisely?

Kate drained her coffee and could think of no reason to prolong the visit. 'I should be going,' she said.

'I hope you'll come again,' said Clare. 'It's good to meet someone from the outside world, if you know what I mean.'

'Well, we're doing our best to integrate. And I will come again. It's been lovely to meet you.'

'Likewise.' Clare looked sad. 'I haven't got much physical movement these days, but I miss very little, you know.'

'I believe you,' Kate said truthfully as she packed up her bag.

There was a definite feeling of tension in the house and Kate was glad to leave.

She wouldn't be ruling out Dickie Payne from her list of suspects.

12

Kate got home, kicked off her shoes and poured herself a glass of Merlot. She leaned back in her chair, trying to relax and empty her mind but instead she found herself wondering how to meet Sandra Miller and Jess Davey. She'd had a peek at their old files in the surgery that afternoon. Medical records could provide clues not only to a person's general health but to their history, as had been the case with Maureen Grey. But there was very little on Jess Davey and not much more on Sandra Miller. The only medical problem Sandra appeared to have was a mild form of contact dermatitis, which was brought on by the latex gloves she had to wear for catering purposes.

While she was thinking about Dickie Payne's steely blue eyes, Barney rested his head on Kate's knee, looking up with that sad, hopeful expression that all dogs have. There was no sign of Angie in the house or the 'studio' and so there was nothing for it but to put on her walking shoes, attach the lead to the dog and set off. She hadn't walked up on the cliffs for several days and was keen to have a close look at the house Woody had bought. On the Up, it was called, which it certainly was geographically. It was one in a row of similar cottages adjoining the coastal path up to Penhallion.

The fourth house along, it was a double-fronted cottage similar to their own, with a slated roof and porch, a green-painted front door and a wall covering of what looked like Virginia creeper. It was bordering on chocolate-box twee-ness, apart from the fact it had no front garden and had very dirty windows. Kate didn't like window-cleaning but, nevertheless, if he lived a little nearer she'd have been tempted to soap them down, then hose them or something.

Deep in thought, she and Barney continued their climb to the coastal path. The sea was choppy today with white horses lining the waves against the grey-blue colour of the water. In spite of the cloud the coastal view was as impressive as ever, stretching from Hartland Point in Devon to the north, as far as Trevose Head in the south; miles of cliffs and jagged rocks and pounding surf. There was a magic about the north coast of Cornwall and, looking west, Kate couldn't quite decide whether she was on a latitude with New York, Nova Scotia, or somewhere in between. In all its moods the Atlantic Ocean pounded on, year after year, century after century, making you realise how very insignificant you were in the scheme of things.

She'd only walk for five or ten minutes up here, Kate decided as she let Barney off the lead, and then retrace her steps before it got too dark. The sky was already darkening and gloom was descending on the clifftop. It took her a few moments to decipher the darker shape of someone emerging from the gloom.

Here he was again: *Seymour Barker-Jones!*

Did this man walk the coastal path every single evening? He must surely have had to ferry his dogs down from Higher Tinworthy in his Land Rover, and why would he do that when surely there were lots of walks to be had up on the moors?

'Here you are again, Mrs Palmer,' he said. He gave a brief wave when he saw her.

'I was just thinking the same thing, Mr Barker-Jones. I was wondering why you never seem to walk up on the moors.'

'The moors are too hazardous for my liking. Hidden mine shafts and areas of bog; I lost a dog there once.'

'How dreadful.' Kate paused. 'Incidentally, I met your housekeeper recently. She seems very loyal.'

'Yes, she is.'

'She mentioned how distraught she was when she heard of your wife's death. And how distraught you were. I felt terribly sorry for you.'

Kate noticed him stiffen and then stand up.

'Are you in the habit of sharing patients' confidences, Mrs Palmer?' He glanced at his watch. 'Time I went back. Good evening to you.'

He was right; perhaps she shouldn't have mentioned that.

It was becoming dark very quickly now so Kate headed for home.

'I don't suppose you fancy making up a foursome for a pub quiz at The Tinners Arms tomorrow night?' Sue asked when Kate arrived for work the following morning. 'The couple we were sharing a table with have cancelled so we need two more.'

'Well…' Kate began, desperately trying to dream up an excuse.

'Perhaps you could bring your sister or someone?' Sue persisted. 'I don't want to let Sandra down.'

'Sandra?' Kate suddenly became alert.

'Yes, Sandra Miller from The Atlantic Hotel. She and I often do pub quizzes.'

'Yes, great, I'd like that. I'm sure my sister will come along.'

This was an ideal opportunity to meet Sandra Miller. Kate reckoned Angie might be persuaded to take part so long as her gin glass was kept topped up.

Angie was quite agreeable. 'It'll make a change from The Greedy Gull,' she said.

'You'll have to use your brain, you know,' Kate said, 'but it gives us a chance to get to know a few more of the locals.'

'The last time you said that was when you dragged me to the WI, and look what happened there!' Angie sniffed. 'Could there be yet another killing on pub-quiz night? Hey, that sounds like an Agatha Christie title, doesn't it? *The Killing at the Pub Quiz?*'

'I'm not too sure that Agatha was into pubs and quizzes,' Kate remarked.

Nevertheless, she and Angie duly presented themselves at The Tinners the following evening. The entire pub was laid out with tables for four, each with a notepad and pencil with which to write the answers, plus the predictable bowls of peanuts and crisps.

Kate had a look around as Angie squeezed her way up through the crowds to the bar to get their drinks. The Tinners Arms, unlike The Greedy Gull, had not been subjected to a lick of paint in many a year. There was no wall art in here, the nicotine-stained finishes a reminder of when everyone smoked, the low beams a reminder that people had been considerably shorter four hundred years ago, and the uneven stone floor a reminder that at least one table leg was going to need a beer mat under it to stop everything wobbling.

Sue waved from one of the tables. She was clad in a white sweater and denim skirt, which emphasised her considerable curves. Kate had never seen her out of uniform before. Sue was accompanied by a very tall, well-built dark-haired woman in a scarlet sweater and jeans. She reeked of cigarettes.

'This is my friend Sandra,' Sue said.

Sandra nodded and said, 'You all right?' which Kate had begun to accept as a standard greeting among many of the Cornish.

'Fine,' Kate replied. 'Nice to meet you. This is my sister, Angie,' she added as Angie appeared with the drinks.

'Sandra and her husband own The Atlantic Hotel,' Sue informed them. 'And we've been given Table Four.'

So this was the famous Sandra Miller! *I should surely be able to suss her out a little this evening*, Kate thought.

They found Table Four, where they deposited their drinks and which, true to form, rocked precariously until Sandra worked out which table leg required the beer mat.

Kate studied Sandra as she got back into her seat, sweeping her long black hair away from her face to reveal an aquiline nose and two large, beady brown eyes. She was one of those rare women who tapered downwards from her heavy shoulders and ample bust to a slim waist and hips and skinny legs encased in skinny jeans. There was something slightly disconcerting about her, Kate thought. Even if she hadn't already heard about her ability to knock a rival senseless, she could see that Sandra Miller wasn't someone you'd wish to upset. She noticed a slight rash on Sandra's fingers and Kate remembered – from reading Sandra's medical notes – that she was allergic to latex. Plainly she'd encountered it recently; not unusual for someone working in hospitality.

'Who wants to write the answers?' Sandra slid the notepad across the table in Kate's direction.

'Yes, OK, I'll do it,' Kate agreed hastily.

A thin leathery old man was dropping bits of paper all over the place on the platform at the far end of the bar.

'Oh my God, it's Joey Baintree reading out the questions!' Sandra sighed and rolled her eyes. 'You can never make out a bloody word he says.'

'This should be fun,' Angie muttered, tackling her gin with gusto.

'Why?' asked Kate. 'What's his problem?'

'His problem is that he's three-quarters pissed before he starts, isn't he, Sue?'

Sue nodded. 'Last time I saw him he fell off the stage.'

'Why do they let him do it then?' Angie asked.

'Because he's the landlord's brother-in-law, that's why, and he's put a lot of money into this place,' Sandra replied. 'And anyway, no one else will do it.' She knocked back a good half of the pint of cider in front of her.

In spite of his failings, Joey Baintree had managed to pick up the papers he'd dropped, and called out, 'Good evenin', ladeesh an' gentlemen! Not that there's many *gentle*men around, ha ha!' He winked at no one in particular and paused, waiting for laughter. None came. 'Sh'pose it's time we got started.'

'Get on with it then, Joey!' someone in the far corner yelled.

'Right-o,' said Joey, consulting his list. 'Firsht section is about geog…' He squinted at the list.

'Geophysics, is it, Joey?' someone else called out, followed by some raucous laughter.

'Nah,' said Joey, composing himself. 'Geography. Can you all 'ear me?'

'Yeah, yeah, get on with it.'

'Next queshtion – do everyone know where the toilets is? For them what don't *know* they's through that door over there, and turn *right*.'

'Only if you're a *bloke*,' a woman shouted out. 'The ladies is on the *left*.'

'Is that the first geography question, Joey?' asked someone on Table Seven.

There were some snorts of laughter before the hapless Joey cleared his throat and said, 'Queshtion one – wot is the capital of Alashka?'

'*Where?*' asked a chorus of people.

He hiccupped. 'Alashka.'

'Oh, Alaska,' someone translated.

Everyone then huddled together with whispers and arguments as to what that could be.

'Anchorage?' Kate whispered hopefully.

'No,' Sue whispered back, 'I've got a feeling it's Fairbanks.'

'Fairbanks? Where did you get that from?' asked Sandra. 'Doesn't sound very Alaskan.'

'It's Juneau,' said Angie firmly.

'Never heard of it,' Kate muttered.

'Juneau,' Angie repeated. 'Write it down.'

Kate did.

They then ploughed their way through obscure mountain ranges, unheard-of rivers and capital cities. Only Angie knew that the capital of Eritrea was Asmara, and that lithosphere was a layer of the earth's crust. Kate stared at her sister in amazement. How did she *know* stuff like that? Was it the gin?

'I just read a lot,' Angie said. 'And I like geography.'

'You can come again,' Sue said, 'can't she, Sandra?'

Sandra, who was draining the last of her cider, was glaring at someone at the next table. She stood up suddenly and shouted at Joey, 'Dora Wally's *cheating*! She's on her mobile under the table googling answers!'

Dora Wally, a buxom blonde with strange black eyebrows, yelled back, 'I am *not*! I was only texting my lad to tell him his dinner's in the oven, so mind your own business, Sandra Miller!'

'No, you bloody *weren't*!' Sandra shouted back. 'You were looking up answers, just like you did that night at Boscastle!'

'Are you calling me a liar?'

'Yes, I am,' Sandra snapped, pushing back her chair.

'This is getting interesting,' Angie murmured to Kate. 'I'm ever so glad I came.'

'Ladeesh, ladeesh!' Joey could barely make himself heard over the babble of conversation. He sat down and wiped his brow. Finally, Roger Finn, the landlord, who'd been blessed with a voice like a foghorn, got up on the platform and called out, 'Settle down, everyone, please! Thank you, Joey, but I'll take over now. Put away

your phone, Mrs Wally! No phones allowed; you *know* the rules!
Sit down, ladies, we don't want any trouble in here!'

Giving each other a final glare, both women were eventually
persuaded to sit down.

'She does that *every* time,' Sandra growled, her dark eyes blazing.
'She should be banned from pub quizzes. Of course she's thick as two
short planks, otherwise she wouldn't need to be cheating, would she?'

Finally, everyone quietened down and Roger resumed the questions. The next section was about sport, which caused much grief
at Table Four since none of them were very clued-up about which
team had won which cup in which league in 2000, or who'd won
the men's doubles at Wimbledon in 2017. And Sandra was only
concentrating on glaring at Dora Wally.

At the end of each round of questions the answers were passed
to the next table for marking. Table Four marked Table Three's
answers, Table Five marked Table Four's, and so on, before the
papers were handed back.

At the end of the general knowledge round Sandra was on her
feet again. 'You've marked us as having *six* out of ten, and we had
seven!' she shouted at Table Five.

'Sorry,' someone at Table Five said.

'I notice *you're* not apologising, Dora Wally,' Sandra said loudly.
'And I expect *you* did the marking.'

'Now, now,' Roger called out, 'I've adjusted the scores on the
blackboard here, ladies. Let's all calm down! Now, IT'S TIME
FOR A BREAK! Refill your glasses, folks, and we'll start again in
fifteen minutes. OK?'

There was much scuffling of chairs and a general rush towards
the bar.

'God, I'm gasping for a smoke,' Sandra said. 'If you hear any
screaming it'll be me murdering someone!' She guffawed as she got

up from the table and headed outside. *Was she referring to Dora Wally, or the murder of Fenella?* Kate wondered briefly.

Angie joined the surge towards the bar, leaving Kate and Sue at the table.

'Sorry about the dramatics,' Sue said. 'Sandra's got a bit of a temper. But Dora Wally really does cheat. She's been caught at it several times and she's been banned from some places.'

'Well, I'm finding it very entertaining,' Kate said with a grin. 'Have you known Sandra long?'

'We were at school together,' Sue said. 'Sandra was always a bit of a rebel. She was very popular with the boys though, and she probably could have married *anyone* but' – here she lowered her voice – 'Ed Miller got her pregnant. Still, she did all right for herself because that hotel's a real money-spinner. And, hey, your sister's a bit of a brainbox, isn't she?'

'No one's more surprised than me,' Kate said. 'She does read a lot though, and it plainly pays off.'

At this point Angie returned with the drinks, and Sandra appeared clutching another pint of cider and brushing cigarette ash off her jumper.

As Sandra tackled her drink she said, 'She was *always* a cow, that Dora Wally.' She nodded towards Table Five. She leaned forward and lowered her voice. 'Have you *seen* those eyebrows? Would you believe she paid a fortune to have those things tattooed on?'

Angie almost choked on her gin. 'She had them tattooed on like that?'

'It's the *thing* at the moment,' Sue said, 'but I think the tattooist must have got carried away!'

'Serve her bloody right!' added Sandra with feeling. 'Two more black marks against her!'

Kate had no idea if the unfortunate Dora Wally was the epitome of awfulness that Sandra had made her out to be, but she was certainly aware of the violent streak in Sandra's nature.

And Sandra wasn't finished yet. She leaned across the table and whispered to Kate and Angie, 'Even when she was in school Dora Wally would drop her knickers for anyone and everyone.'

'Oh,' Kate said politely, wondering if Dora had dropped them for the French chef. Was that why Sandra hated her so much?

'Almost as bad as bloody Fenella Barker-Jones,' Sandra summed up, just as the second half of the quiz was about to begin.

There were no further incidents. At the end of the quiz Table Four had scored one point more than Table Five, much to Kate's relief, as she could imagine a battle taking place otherwise. They were positioned somewhere in the middle in the final tally.

'At least we didn't come last,' Sue said as she put on her coat. 'Thank you both for coming along. Perhaps we can do this another time? We're very impressed with your knowledge, Angie. And you too, Kate,' she added. Kate made a non-committal noise. If nothing else this evening she had learned that a female moose is a cow, that Mammolo was a red wine grape, that a bombardon was a musical instrument and that *Pictures at an Exhibition* was a piece of music written by Mussorgsky. And that Sandra Miller was a fiery lady who, Kate suspected, could quite possibly stick a knife into someone she disliked.

As they got into the car Angie said, 'Do they ever have any *normal* events round here? I mean where nobody gets knifed or comes close to having a stand-up fight? Pub quizzes used to be respectable events, did they not?'

'They did,' Kate agreed, still seeing the fury in Sandra Miller's eyes.

She was another one who would be remaining on The List.

13

Kate worried about how Maureen was coping since being hauled into the police station. Gossip spread like wildfire in a place like Tinworthy and no doubt tongues would be wagging wherever she went. As she tried to work out what excuse she could make to visit her someone knocked on the door, which set the dog off into hysterical barking.

The tall skinny lad who'd arrived on the doorstep of Lavender Cottage didn't look much older than sixteen.

He held out an ID card in a bony hand. 'Jordan Jarvis,' he said, 'from the *Cornish Courier*.'

Kate had seen some members of the press hanging around in the lane and approaching her when she got into her car, but this was the first time that somebody had actually come to the door.

'Sorry,' she said, 'I don't…'

'*Please!*' he begged. There was something about the way his Adam's apple bobbed up and down above his black polo neck that made Kate hesitate just long enough for him to add, 'This is my first big job, see? My auntie lives in the village and she said how nice you were and that you'd found the bodies and everything.'

His manner, if not his looks, reminded her of Jack. Then he smiled hopefully and she noticed he had beautiful teeth. He also had a very red nose and he was shivering. Kate had been advised by Woody to avoid the press at all costs, but there was something about this boy.

'Come in for a minute,' she said, standing to one side. 'You look frozen.'

He followed her into the kitchen, dumped his backpack on the floor and headed straight for the log burner to warm his hands. 'Nice and warm in here,' he said, sniffing.

'I'm not sure what I can do for you, Jordan,' Kate said. 'I've absolutely nothing to say to the press. But you look so cold! Would you like a hot drink?'

'Oh, I could murder a cup of tea,' he replied, then clamped his hand over his mouth. 'I shouldn't have said that, should I, with all those murders going on round here?'

Kate smiled as she filled up the kettle and got out a couple of mugs. 'How old are you, Jordan?'

Jordan had pulled out a chair and seated himself at the kitchen table.

'I'm eighteen,' he said, 'and I might be a junior reporter at the moment but I've got big plans. One day I'm going to be working for *The Times* or *The Guardian* or one of the national papers in London. But you have to start somewhere, don't you? Can I have milk and three sugars, please?'

'I'm sure you'll do well, Jordan,' Kate said as she stirred his tea and handed him the mug.

'And I want to be a crime reporter,' he went on, taking a gulp of his tea, 'so aren't I lucky that all *this* is going on locally? Couldn't be better! I managed to persuade them to let me cover this story so I've got to come up with *something*.'

Kate knew that the *Cornish Courier* didn't have a huge circulation, unlike most of its better-known rivals.

'The old hacks are all hanging around up at the police station in Launceston,' he said, 'and they take the piss out of me, but I'm going to show them.'

'No doubt you will,' Kate said as she watched him slurp his tea, his nose slowly returning to its normal pink.

'There's a load of them down the lane there,' he said, 'but I sneaked away when they weren't looking. The thing is, Mrs Palmer, we're not supposed to bother you cos we get handouts from the police every so often but, to be honest, they don't seem to have much clue. But they've got some woman under arrest, I'm told.'

'And do you think I do? Have a clue?' Kate asked.

'Well, that's what I'd like to find out, because you found the bodies, didn't you?'

'I found Kevin Barry but I wasn't first on the scene with Mrs Barker-Jones,' Kate informed him.

'But you must know everyone round here and who'd be likely to do it?'

'Strangely enough I don't. I've only lived here for a couple of months.'

Kate noticed a drip forming on the end of his nose and, seeing him about to disperse it with the back of his hand, she grabbed a tissue and handed it to him.

'Oh thanks,' he said, giving his nose a hearty blow. 'The hacks all reckon it's that Grey couple who did it. There's a load of press up there outside the house waiting for one of them to come out.'

'I wouldn't be too sure of anything yet,' Kate said, watching with some amusement as he withdrew a tatty notebook out of his bag and searched in vain for a pen.

'Here you are,' she said, handing him a biro. She couldn't help liking the lad, although she felt he had a considerable journey ahead of him before he got to the dizzy heights of reporting for *The Times* or *The Guardian*.

'So,' he said, pen poised, 'you've only been here a couple of months and you've had to deal with *two* bodies!'

'That's about it,' Kate agreed, then added with a wink, 'but it wasn't *me* whodunnit!'

He grinned at her as he drained his mug. 'Could I write a little piece about you, Mrs Palmer? How you came to live here from, er, where?'

'West London,' Kate replied.

'Wow! So you come from great big London to a tiddly Cornish village and straight away you're surrounded by dead bodies! How cool is that!'

'That's a slight exaggeration.' Kate was beginning to wonder if it had been wise to let Jordan over the doorstep. 'It's only because I'm a nurse that they asked me to have a look at Mrs Barker-Jones's body.'

'But what about the Barry bloke?'

'Ah well, yes, I found him washed up on the beach.'

'That wouldn't have happened up in London now, would it?' he asked, frantically scribbling.

'We're a bit short of beaches up in London,' Kate agreed. 'Anyway, that was pure chance while I was walking the dog.'

Jordan laid down the pen and studied her with a very serious expression. 'No, Mrs Palmer,' he said, 'I don't think it was. I think it's a *sign*. I think it was a sign that you're *meant* to be involved in all this.' He was now becoming quite excited. 'I'm a great believer in signs.'

'I fear it was purely coincidence,' Kate said, panicking slightly about what sort of piece he was planning to write, 'so please don't go putting stuff about signs into this article of yours. Really, the less you say about me the better.'

'OK,' he said, writing again. 'Is there any more tea?'

He's not short of nerve, Kate thought. But he hadn't sounded cheeky so she preferred to think he was just thirsty.

As she refilled his mug he said, 'I like to get the human angle, you see. Like how do you feel about coming down here and landing yourself in the middle of all this?'

'Surprised,' Kate replied. 'It certainly isn't how I imagined life would be here.'

'Did you ever have to deal with murders up in London?' he asked.

'I did occasionally have to deal with stabbings and knife crimes from time to time when I worked in Accident and Emergency,' she said. 'We patched people up as well as we could and sometimes they recovered, sometimes they didn't. You just have to cope with it.'

'Wow!' he exclaimed admiringly. 'Haven't you had an exciting life!'

'Just the average life of a nurse,' Kate said. She'd never considered her life to be particularly exciting, but she was amused and a little flattered by this young man's interest and enthusiasm.

'So,' he said, 'do you have any idea who the murderer might be?'

'None at all,' she replied truthfully, thinking of The List and how she'd not yet felt like crossing any of the names off.

He asked her a few questions about her marital status – had she children, grandchildren?

'Well, I'd better leave you in peace now,' he said finally, stowing away his notebook and *her* pen into his bag. 'Thanks ever so much for the chat and for the tea, Mrs Palmer. I'll make sure you get a copy of the *Cornish Courier*.'

'Good luck, Jordan,' Kate said as she shepherded him out the door, wondering what on earth she'd let herself in for.

14

The following day Woody phoned. For a few heart-stopping moments Kate wondered if he'd heard that she'd been talking to the press and was about to chastise her.

'Maureen Grey's off the hook for the moment,' he said.

'Thank God for that. Why?'

'Because her husband, Billy, walked into the police station yesterday and confessed to committing both murders.'

Kate was dumbstruck for a moment. 'He did?'

'He did. So now he's been charged and is in detention.'

'Oh, Woody, I'm so relieved Maureen's no longer a suspect. But do you really think he did it?'

'Well, he confessed, so we have no option but to believe him.'

'But why are you calling me and telling me this?' Kate asked.

'Because Maureen Grey has been with us at the police station today and she's asked if you would be kind enough to come and pick her up. We've offered her a police car to take her home but, for some reason, she wants you.'

'Of course I'll come to collect her!' Kate felt flattered that Maureen had finally come to trust her. 'You must be relieved you've got the killer.'

'Yes,' Woody replied, not sounding altogether convinced. 'Though Maureen's still not to leave the area, I know you're fond of her and I think she's probably rather short of friends at the moment.'

'Oh, poor Maureen!'

'Yeah, I thought you'd want to know.'

'Thanks, Woody. I'll be there shortly to pick her up.'

*

Maureen stood, waif-like, with a small bag on the ground beside her, outside the entrance to the police station. Kate's heart lurched. This poor woman!

'Oh, Maureen,' she said, as she parked the car, got out and opened the passenger door. 'I'm so glad you're not a suspect anymore.'

Maureen sniffed as she got into the car. 'Well, it's thanks to you telling that detective about me and Kevin in the churchyard that made them think it was me.'

'I'm sorry, Maureen. But I felt it was relevant at the time.'

'Did you now?' Maureen said. 'Anyway, can you stop at the next petrol station so I can get some milk for my tea?'

'Of course I can.'

Kate drove on, aware that Maureen wasn't in a conversational mood. They stopped for milk and then drove on in companionable silence for the remainder of the short journey to St Petroc's Road.

Maureen pursed her lips as she opened the door. 'You'd better come in then,' she said ungraciously, 'but I don't want any lectures from you.'

'I don't lecture,' Kate protested, 'and if I sound as if I do then I'm sorry.'

She followed Maureen into the living room where she stooped to put on the electric fire. A piece of cream-coloured knitting had been abandoned on one of the fireside chairs.

'What's this you're knitting?' Kate asked as she held up the length of cable stitching.

'A jumper,' Maureen said as she filled up the kettle.

'For yourself?'

'No.' Maureen volunteered no further information which made Kate wonder if it could possibly be for the husband. She decided not to ask.

'Wish I could knit like this,' she said instead.

Maureen came back into the room. 'Sit down,' she said, indicating the other chair. Then she picked up the knitting, sat down opposite, and resumed knitting at top speed, as if she'd only placed it down a few minutes ago.

'Did you know, Maureen? Did you know he'd killed Fenella and Kevin?'

'No,' Maureen said as she got up again to make the tea, 'because I don't think he did.'

'*What?* Why do you say that?' Kate was becoming increasingly confused. Had she heard correctly?

'How do I know that you won't tell everything I say to that detective friend of yours?'

'I won't!' How did Maureen know she was friendly with Woody? Kate was nevertheless torn between her wish to help Woody solve the case and keeping Maureen's trust. She decided instantly she had to keep Maureen's trust. 'Honestly, I promise,' she added. 'But, Maureen, I'm very confused. The last time I sat in here you were telling me how awful your husband was and that you'd shut the door in his face.'

'I did,' Maureen agreed, handing Kate a mug of very strong tea. 'I *did* shut the door in his face. After ten bloody years what did he expect? That I'd give him a hug and say, "Welcome home!" Are you *kidding?*'

'No, but you must have let him in at some point. According to all reports he has been living here.'

'Yes,' said Maureen. She sipped her tea and picked up the knitting yet again. 'I did let him in after he broke down. He broke down on the doorstep, would you believe. There were curtains twitching all the way down the road so I couldn't have all that going on outside my house. He said he hadn't been able to cope with losing Lucy and then me being put in the loony bin. You know I was sectioned at Bodmin, don't you?'

'Yes,' Kate said, 'but you must have been so stricken with grief that you didn't know what you were doing.'

'Oh, I knew what I was doing all right. I nearly killed Billy with a bread knife. What is it with knives in this place?' Maureen seemed bemused for a moment. 'And so they put me away.'

'And Billy took off,' Kate prompted.

'Yeah, Billy took off. Can't blame him, I suppose. He went up to London, you know.'

Kate nodded and drank her tea.

'Then,' Maureen continued, 'he gets this woman pregnant. Just like that!' The needles continued clicking furiously. 'Did you know that it took me five years to get pregnant after Billy and I were married? *Five* bloody years! And this woman gets pregnant *first time*! Where's the justice in that?'

Kate shook her head in commiseration. 'There's no justice in the world, Maureen.'

'And then,' Maureen said, 'she has a little girl and she wants Billy to move in with her. So the silly bugger does just that, not bothering to tell her that he's married.' She looked at Kate with tears in her eyes. 'He has a little girl. *Another* little girl.'

'Oh, Maureen, I'm sorry. That must be awful for you. Cruel.'

'He told me everything. Said he was sorry and that he'd come back to put things right. That's what he said. Begged forgiveness. Because he got a letter from Kevin Barry too, you know, saying that it had been Fenella driving and not him.'

'How did Kevin know where Billy was?' Kate asked.

'He didn't. He sent it to his girlfriend, Jess Davey, and asked her to take it to Billy's mother to forward on. She still lives up in Higher Tee, you know. She's not a bad old bird, tried to help me back then but I didn't want her anywhere near. Anyway, she sent the letter on to Billy in London. Billy stayed with her a couple of nights after I sent him away, but they got on each other's nerves. They've always been rowing, never really got on.'

'So, if Billy knew it was Fenella who was driving, why would he have killed Kevin too?'

'He said he waited until Kevin Barry got out of jail because he wanted to knock seven bells out of him, that's what he said.'

'Even though Kevin wasn't driving?'

'He felt the same way I did. It was one of them – him covering up for her, her covering up for him – who knows?'

'So he came back to kill them both?'

'That's what he told the police,' Maureen said drily.

'But you don't think he did, even though he's admitted it to the police?'

'He said he wanted to prove how sorry he was about everything. I got a feeling he confessed so they wouldn't keep harassing me.'

'Oh my God!' Kate didn't know what to think. If he'd actually admitted it, then surely…? 'I can't believe this. He'll get life, won't he?'

Maureen shrugged. There was silence for a few minutes apart from Maureen's knitting needles clicking away. It seemed to keep her calm and Kate thought it might provide some sort of comfort, like worry beads.

'Imagine him having another little girl,' Maureen said eventually. 'I wonder if she looks like him? Lucy looked like him, you know. Do you think she might look like Lucy?'

'Don't torture yourself thinking about it,' Kate said.

'It's not the little girl's fault.' Maureen laid down her knitting. 'More tea?'

'No thanks.'

Maureen resumed knitting. 'Her name is Jasmine. The little girl.'

'That's a pretty name.' Kate could sense that Maureen had an understandable fascination with Billy's new family, at least for the little daughter. She'd hardly mentioned the woman at all.

'I expect they'll put Billy in Dartmoor,' Maureen said matter-of-factly. 'That's where Kevin Barry was. I hope so because it's closer. I could get someone to drive me there, couldn't I?'

'Yes, if you wanted to see him,' Kate said.

'Well, *of course* I'd want to if he was taking the blame.'

'But you *definitely* don't think he did it?' Kate persisted. 'Because if he didn't, then there's at least one killer who's getting away with it, and who could strike again. You *must* tell the police about your doubts.'

Maureen stared at her for a moment, pursed her lips and said nothing.

'Is there anything I can do to help?' Kate asked after a short silence.

'Like what?'

'I don't know. *Anything*. You can call me anytime. Best to ring me on my mobile though. Have you still got my card?'

Maureen nodded.

Kate stood up. 'OK, I'll leave you in peace then, but don't forget I'm here if you need me.'

Maureen laid down her knitting again and accompanied Kate to the door. 'I suppose you mean well,' she said with the ghost of a smile as she ushered Kate out.

Kate stood outside for a few minutes listening to the key being turned in the lock and the chain being rattled into place.

15

When Kate arrived home Angie was standing in the hallway clutching the saucepan.

'So, you're back then.'

'Yes, I'm back.'

'And how's the murderess?'

'She's not a murderess,' Kate replied emphatically.

'I don't know why you make such a fuss about that woman,' Angie said. 'You've only seen her a couple of times so how you can be so sure she's innocent?'

'I just have a feeling about Maureen,' Kate replied. 'She's found out what that so-called husband of hers has been up to in his absence.'

'Really?'

'Yes, apparently he's been living with some woman in London somewhere, and they have a daughter. Can you believe it?'

'Of course I believe it. What did you expect him to do, live in a monastery?'

'Anyway, he's confessed to the murders and been arrested, so obviously it *isn't* Maureen.'

'Maybe she's just let him take the rap to punish him,' said Angie.

Kate sighed. 'You're so bloody insensitive at times!' she snapped. She had no intention of telling Angie about her conversation with Maureen.

'I'm not insensitive. I simply cannot work out why you think she's so saintly when she had just as much motive as he had to see off both Fenella and Kevin.'

Kate didn't bother to answer. But, deep down, she'd been think-ing along similar lines. Perhaps the husband had reappeared purely to help Maureen dispose of Fenella and Kevin?

Could they be in it together?

She needed to clear her head and to get out into the fresh air. 'Come on, Barney!' she yelled and the dog, who'd been fast asleep in front of the stove, leaped to his feet, tail wagging manically.

Off they set, down to the river, across the bridge and up towards the coastal path. There was a path on the south side too, above Lavender Cottage, but it was stony, steep and with rough steps cut into the rock that could be hazardous. All in all, Kate had decided early on that the north side was the better bet.

Kate hadn't seen Seymour the last couple of times she'd walked up there, and there was no sign of him today, so she sat on the seat and gazed out to sea. There were no tankers on the horizon, only one small fishing boat, bobbing up and down on the waves. Kate sat for around fifteen minutes, thinking deeply about whether Seymour should be on her list.

Seymour Barker-Jones was an enigmatic character, no doubt about that. She wondered if the rumours she'd heard about him being with MI5 were true; she could well believe it because he was such a difficult person to read.

He had looked sad when she'd seen him last so surely he'd had deep feelings for his wife even if he wasn't around very much? Surely at some time he must have loved Fenella? Though had anybody *really* loved Fenella? With the string of affairs she'd had it was clear she was searching for something. Perhaps the reason Fenella had had all these affairs was to compensate for her husband never being around? That's what Kate would like to think, though of course life was rarely that simple.

Kate felt sorry for the woman, who appeared to have had people queuing up to finish her off.

And now Billy Grey had admitted to the crimes. Was Maureen involved? Could she be guilty of aiding and abetting on either or both of the killings? Kate's gut feeling was that she was not. And what about Billy's family in London? Had he come back on the tenth anniversary of Lucy's death – immediately after Kevin's release from prison – just to murder him and Fenella? He had confessed to being the killer. And yet…

Then Kate wondered if she was on the wrong track altogether. What about Sandra Miller? There was no doubt whatsoever that you wouldn't want to cross that woman. She seemed a volatile and unpredictable character who might well have had reason to kill Fenella. But *Kevin*?

Kate continued to mull it over as she walked back down the hill towards home.

Angie – who for some reason was all dolled up this evening – offered Kate a gin and tonic the moment she walked through the door.

As she handed her the glass she said, 'I've been thinking about your list. Is Maureen's husband the guilty one? I'm still not sure that we haven't got a serial killer around, which is what I said in the first place.'

'But,' Kate said, 'if this serial killer of yours is looking for any passing female to plunge a knife into, then why did he kill Kevin by bashing him on the side of his head and then drowning him?'

'Well, maybe one of the Greys killed Kevin.'

'Why are you suddenly being so helpful and why are you all dressed up?'

'Actually, I'm off out, so don't wait up.'

Kate glanced at her watch. Six thirty. 'Are you planning five hours at the pub?'

'No, I'm off on a date with lovely Luke of The Gallery fame. He's going to show me his art collection, take me out for a meal and we may end up at The Gull for a nightcap later. And your jaw just dropped to the floor!'

Kate was astounded. '*Luke?* How long has this little affair been going on then?'

'It isn't an affair. Not yet. But you must admit he's quite fanciable. Don't tell me he's on your bloody list!'

'Of course he's not on my list! But, I mean, isn't he a little *young* for you, Angie?'

'You're as young as you feel.' Angie replied airily, applying lipstick and surveying herself with some satisfaction in her handbag mirror. 'See you later!'

And she was gone.

Kate sat down to ponder this piece of news. She knew of course that Angie had met Luke several times in the pub, and that she was hopeful he would display some of her artwork in The Gallery. But going out on a date with a guy who looked young enough to be her *son*? Perhaps he was older than he looked. And these things didn't seem to bother Angie so good luck to her!

Kate didn't hear Angie return from her date as she'd gone to bed early. For no accountable reason she found herself wide awake at four o'clock. She listened to Angie's snoring through the wall as sleep continued to elude her and finally, at six, she gave up and went downstairs to make a cup of tea.

Although she was curious to know how her sister had got on with Luke, she knew Angie would be unlikely to surface before mid-morning. Had he been persuaded to display and stock her canvases? Kate knew little about modern art and had never failed to be surprised at the prices some of these weird and wonderful abstract squiggles achieved. Perhaps she was underestimating Angie? Nevertheless, Kate couldn't visualise any of them adorning the walls of the cottage and fortunately Angie had never suggested such a thing. *I'll cross that bridge when I come to it*, Kate thought.

As she popped bread into the toaster she thought of Woody. Apart from her evening out at The Edge of the Moor with him, she hadn't been out with any man in the last couple of years. Yes, Woody was extremely 'fanciable', as Angie put it and, best of all, he seemed to be as taken with her as she was with him. When this case was over and he was retired from the CID perhaps they could finally have a proper relationship? Of course he might only regard it as a platonic friendship – and it wasn't as if she was *looking* for a partner, and certainly not a husband! Never again!

Angie appeared at half past ten, in her dressing gown, yawning. 'I love Saturday mornings,' she said as she filled up the kettle.

'I can't see why Saturday mornings are different from any other mornings for you,' Kate remarked. 'It's not as if you have to go out to work.'

'It's psychological then, I expect,' said Angie, 'remembering how it used to be.'

Kate decided not to remind her that during her acting career Saturdays had been the busiest day of the week with a matinee as well as an evening performance.

'How did you get on with Luke?' she asked instead.

'Good, very good,' Angie replied. 'He showed me all round The Gallery and he's got some lovely artwork, plus fabulous pottery and jewellery. At the moment he's only open weekends, but he'll be open every day from Easter onwards. Which is only a week away, I see.' She studied the calendar on the wall.

'That'll keep him busy then,' Kate remarked. 'So, what else did you do? Go for a meal?'

'He lives in the flat above The Gallery, so we went up there because he'd made us a vegetable chilli, which was delicious.'

'A vegetable chilli, eh? Is he—'

'Yeah, he's vegetarian,' Angie interrupted. 'Says you have to travel miles to find decent veggie food in a restaurant, so he doesn't bother. And of course meat's expensive and don't forget he hardly earns any money all winter.'

'And then what did you do?'

'And then we went to The Gull for a nightcap or two. It was a lovely evening. And later he's coming over to the studio to see my canvases. I'm so excited! I hope to God he likes them.'

'Well, good luck with that,' Kate said. 'You've worked hard so I hope he'll be impressed.' She didn't know anything about modern art so perhaps they really were masterpieces.

As Angie sat down with her mug of tea she said, 'I might help him out in The Gallery during the summer sometimes when it's busy.'

'Doing what?'

'Selling stuff, chatting to customers, all that sort of thing. It'll be easy because everything's price-tagged and he'll show me how to work the till because it's all computerised these days, you know.'

'And what's he planning to pay you?'

'Oh, it's *vulgar* to talk about money with a friend. It's not important anyway,' Angie said airily. 'It'll just be so lovely to be part of the *art world* and surrounded by beautiful things.'

'Including yours?'

'Hopefully. Wouldn't that be *wonderful?*'

Kate hadn't seen her sister look so bright-eyed or excited in years. Angie had always been gullible, but if this arrangement made her happy, so be it. It might even keep her off the gin because – if she remembered correctly – most establishments in Lower Tinworthy stayed open until late into the evening during the summer.

'Anyway,' said Angie, plunging her mug into the sink, 'I must go now as I have lots to do before Luke gets here this evening. Must tart up the art!' she guffawed. 'Hopefully he'll like one of them sufficiently to display it, maybe even *sell* it!'

Oh, he'll certainly display it, Kate thought, *because he'll want you to be running the shop, probably unpaid, any time he fancies a day off. And, if he does pay anything at all, it'll be peanuts.*

It was late evening before Luke appeared and the two of them disappeared into the 'studio' before heading towards The Greedy Gull.

The following morning Angie came bounding down the stairs. 'Luke *loves* my work,' she said triumphantly to Kate, 'and he's going to stock one of my large canvases. Probably the Indian Summer one.'

Kate was mystified. 'Indian Summer? Since when did your pictures have names?'

'Since last night,' Angie replied. 'There's Cornish Spring, and Midwinter Blues, and I've still to think up some names for the others. Indian Summer is the one that's predominantly reds and golds.'

'Oh,' said Kate.

'He may even display it in the window,' said Angie. 'And I'm going to be helping him in The Gallery right over the Easter weekend and then – once I've got the hang of everything – I'll be able to do the occasional day there on my own.'

'Hmmm,' said Kate, 'and has he said yet what's he planning to pay you?'

'Oh God, Kate, I keep telling you it's so *vulgar* to talk about money. I've no doubt we'll come to some arrangement eventually. Any word from the dishy detective?'

'Until this case is completely wound up we mustn't be seeing each other.' Kate sighed.

'So *that's* why you're so intent on solving these murders!' Angie snorted.

Perhaps she's right, Kate thought.

16

Wednesday afternoon was clear and sunny with not a cloud in the sky. After Kate got home, changed and downed a cup of tea, she decided it was a perfect day for viewing the coastline from the clifftops. Barney was definitely taken with the idea when he saw Kate go to fetch his lead, barking enthusiastically and manically tail-wagging.

Even the normally fuzzy outline of Lundy Island, twelve miles off the North Devon coast, was crystal clear in the afternoon sunshine and the coastline and cliffs in both directions were so sharply defined that Kate thought she could see gulls perched on their ledges more than a mile away.

As she walked up and along the coastal path, she spotted Seymour on that seat again, gazing out to sea.

'Clear as a bell today,' he greeted her.

She sat down on the far end of the seat, glad to rest her aching muscles after the long upward climb. 'It is,' she said.

'But no boats on the horizon.'

'No,' she agreed.

'Sometimes,' he said, 'I'd like to get on a boat and sail away myself. Never touch base, just sail on and on. Escapism, I suppose.'

'And what do you feel you have to escape from?' Kate said.

'The horror of my wife's death,' he said, turning to look at her. There was a sadness and loneliness about the man that intrigued Kate.

'It *was* horrific,' she agreed. 'I can't imagine how someone could do that to another human being. It's such a terrible thing. Do you really believe Billy Grey is the killer?'

He hesitated. 'Yes, of course.' He continued gazing out to sea.

Kate wasn't sure she believed him. 'Now they've made an arrest you'll be able to get away. It must be important for you to get back to your work in London,' she said.

'Yes, it is.' He turned to look at her. 'But it's more important to me that this whole horrible business is finally wrapped up.'

'It must have been heartbreaking for you,' Kate said, 'and frustrating.'

'Did you know my wife?' he asked.

'No, I didn't,' Kate admitted. 'But I do feel involved. You see, I was at the meeting when she was killed and because I'm a nurse I was called to check on her. Then, six days later I found Kevin Barry's body washed up on the beach.'

Seymour looked horrified. 'My God! How awful for you! You *have* become involved, haven't you?'

Kate felt the need to confide. 'It was awful, but it's galvanised me into finding out who committed these awful crimes.'

Seymour gave a glimmer of a smile. 'Is that so?'

'Yes, you see, I've made a list of suspects…' Kate trailed off, immediately wondering if it had been wise to tell him that.

'And am I on it?' he asked.

She most definitely should *not* have started this conversation.

'Because I should be,' he went on, 'if you're being thorough.' He was studying her intently. 'But don't you think you can tear up your list now?'

Kate hesitated. 'I suppose I should,' she said.

'You don't sound altogether convinced?'

'I just think there's a bit more to this than meets the eye. Perhaps I watch too many detective dramas.' Kate wondered again if she was saying too much.

'So why are you not convinced?'

Kate shrugged. 'Just a feeling I have. And my feelings are usually correct – more by luck than judgement probably. Let's just say that I can't say for certain that it's all wrapped up. I shall keep my list for the moment.'

'And yet the police are satisfied that this man Grey is the killer, aren't they?'

'It would seem so.'

'Good,' he said. He looked sad again as he gazed back out to sea. 'But nothing can bring her back.'

As he stood up to go he said, 'Everyone will tell you that we lived separate lives and that, of course, is true. Fenella hated London and unfortunately I have to be there most of the time. Alas, I was not the husband she was hoping for. I was unable to fulfil all her needs, but I loved my wife and I miss her.' He looked round and whistled for his dogs. 'Good day, Mrs Palmer.'

And, with that, he was gone, the dogs running ahead.

Kate mulled over her meeting with Seymour as she walked back home. He was indeed an enigmatic character but nevertheless she found herself drawn to him a little. What did he mean when he said he wasn't the husband Fenella was hoping for? Rumour had it that he was bisexual, gay, impotent even, so perhaps he'd been unable to satisfy her in that department? Perhaps Fenella needed to prove to herself that she was attractive to men and that was why she took so many lovers? Then again she may well have been unashamedly voracious, and she and Seymour might well have had an open marriage. Kate was tempted to erase Seymour – along with Maureen and Jess – from The List, but she didn't. She would erase him once it was proved beyond doubt who the killer was.

But she was none too sure that killer was Billy Grey.

*

The very next day all roads heading to the South West were grid-locked with Easter tourists who'd managed to begin their weekend a day early. And Kate finally realised that what the old girl up the lane had forecast was true: there was a constant stream of visitors walking up the lane and peering into the back garden. Fortunately, the little garden at the front – overlooking the valley and the sea – was reasonably private unless you walked along the side of the house and looked over the gate which was set in the hedge.

'Luke says there are far more visitors than usual,' Angie informed Kate as she ran her fingers through her topknot to accentuate the arty look, prior to her stint in The Gallery. 'He says it's because the village is now notorious! Word's got round that a body was found on the beach, and a murder took place in the dreary old village hall, and they're arriving in droves and asking who lives where. I bet someone'll come knocking on the door before long!'

Someone did.

Shortly after Angie departed, Kate was tidying up the kitchen when there was a knock at the back door. And there – clad in anoraks and bobble hats – stood a group of around twenty people, cameras poised at the ready.

'Are you Mrs Palmer?' asked their bespectacled leader. 'I'm Wally. Forgive us for coming to your door like this, but we're the Agatha Christie Commemoration Association from Little Widdlington – that's near Cheltenham – and we *love* to visit crime scenes. We understand you found the body of' – he consulted a scrap of paper – 'er, Mr Kevin Barry, recently released from prison, who'd come back, according to rumour, to murder his former employer?'

Kate was dumbstruck for a few moments while they all continued to gawp at her expectantly and several cameras flashed and clicked.

'I'm sorry, I don't see how I can help you,' she said at last.

'We just wondered how it must have felt, finding the body of a *murdered man*?' Wally persisted. There was a visible shiver of excitement rippling through the entire group.

'Naturally, I was shocked; I contacted the police, and that's about it,' Kate said. 'Now, if you'll excuse me…'

'What sort of state was the body in?' someone near the back asked eagerly.

'Very dead,' Kate replied drily. 'Now, really, there's nothing more to say.'

'The media said that he was killed by a blow to the head before he ended up in the sea,' Wally continued. 'Can you confirm that?'

'I can confirm nothing,' Kate said as she began to close the door. 'You must talk to the police. Thank you.' With that she shut the door firmly, feeling quite shaken. What sort of people would get a kick from visiting murder sites and asking daft questions like that? She'd peer through the side window in future before opening the door.

She experimented by looking out straight away and was relieved to see them all heading back down the lane, led by Wally. None of them looked a day under sixty.

Was this to be the pattern for the months ahead?

Easter Sunday didn't go quite as planned. Kate had bought a leg of lamb to roast for lunch for the two of them, and then Angie decided it was only right that she should be able to invite Luke for lunch.

'Do you really think you should?' Kate asked. 'Doesn't he have any family around?'

'No, he hasn't,' Angie went on, 'and I live here too. It would be a lovely way to thank Luke for all he's done. And why haven't you asked the dishy detective too?'

'The dishy detective's visiting his daughter in London.' Kate was determined not to be sidetracked. 'I thought you said that you had to man The Gallery all day and every day over Easter.'

'Oh, we can shut shop for an hour or so and put a notice on the door saying "Back at 2 p.m." or something. Tell you what,' Angie continued, 'I'll do the dessert. Something lemony, perhaps? No, no, it must be chocolate seeing as it's Easter. I'll tell him about one o'clock then, shall I? Thanks, Kate, I knew you'd agree!'

'But I thought you said he was vegetarian? He won't be able to eat the lamb, will he?'

'Oh, we'll do him some extra vegetables or something. Don't get your knickers in a twist.'

With that Angie – clad in her smock and with her hair carefully tousled again – set off for The Gallery.

When Angie appeared at quarter past one with Luke in tow on Easter Sunday, Kate managed not to do a double-take, because Luke had added some green streaks to his long, bleached-blond hair. Had Angie been chucking paint at him or was it a professional job? He'd swept it back behind his left ear to display a number of ear piercings and several earrings. He too wore an artist's smock in navy blue, artfully splashed with red and white here and there, above which two gold chains could be seen adorning his neck.

'Smells great!' he said, sniffing the air and plonking himself down on the sofa.

'How's The Gallery's doing, Luke? You got many visitors?' Kate asked politely, handing him a glass of wine.

'A few who are really interested,' Luke replied. 'We had loads of them yesterday but I fear they'd only come in to shelter from the rain.'

'So, did anyone buy anything?' Kate asked.

'Just some silver earrings,' Angie said. 'Lovely they were.'

Lunch went without a hitch. The lamb was delicious, the roast potatoes golden, the vegetables crisp. Luke seemed content with his plateful of vegetables, and Angie's chocolate pudding, decorated with tiny Easter eggs, went down a storm. The wine and the conversation flowed, the latter mainly dominated by Luke's long-winded and left-leaning opinion on just about everything, while Angie looked adoringly at him.

'Well,' he concluded, 'at least we can all relax now that the killer's in jail. Mind you, Angie here is still convinced there's a mass murderer on the loose, and I think she's quite disappointed now they've got Grey under lock and key.'

'I'm not sure that they have any real proof though,' Kate said, 'other than his confession.'

'Why would anyone confess if they hadn't done it?' Luke looked at her as if she was mad.

'Perhaps he had his reasons.' Kate hadn't confided to Angie the details of her conversation with Maureen.

'Well, he'd be bloody barmy if he confessed to two murders he hadn't done!' Luke exclaimed. 'Barmy! He'll get life but they'll likely let him out early if he behaves himself. They'll sympathise with him, see, because he was avenging the death of his daughter. It wasn't just because he had the *urge* to kill someone.'

It was half past three before Angie and Luke made their unsteady way back to The Gallery.

So much for the 'Back at 2 p.m.' sign on the door, Kate thought as she collapsed wearily onto the sofa. Luke certainly wouldn't be her choice but nevertheless she felt a little jealous that Angie and he seemed to get on so well. She wished too that Woody had been here today. Maybe next year?

Kate filled the dishwasher and decided both she and Barney had need of some fresh air.

After yesterday's rain, it was sunny as she set off with the dog on the less-favoured route to the cliffs above Lavender Cottage. It was a tougher climb and a rougher terrain, stony and undulating, up to Bugalow Point. They met only an occasional walker, clad in anorak, boots and backpack, and a few groups of tourists. Down below she could see some wetsuit-clad hopefuls struggling with their newly bought bodyboards in the gentle waves. The beach was crowded and the little parade of shops buzzing with tourists. Kate wondered briefly if Angie had managed to sell her painting. Then she wondered how Woody was getting on with his daughter and when she'd see him again.

17

In spite of Woody's warnings Kate was determined to know more about the remaining suspects, Sandra Miller in particular given that she had been outside smoking at the exact time of Fenella's murder. Kate decided she desperately needed to learn something more specific about both Sandra and Dickie Payne in the absence of any leads.

'Angie,' she said, 'how do you fancy afternoon tea tomorrow at The Atlantic Hotel? It's supposed to be very nice.'

'And very expensive,' said Angie. 'So what's brought this on? You're not an afternoon tea sort of person.'

'Well, now we're living down here I might become one. And I just thought it might be nice for us to go out somewhere together other than The Greedy Gull.'

Angie digested this for a minute. 'It wouldn't be anything to do with the fact that Sandra Miller's on that silly list of yours, would it?'

'Oh, for *goodness'* sake! She probably won't even be there,' Kate said dismissively but silently praying that she would be. How else was she to meet this woman again without any pub quizzes in the offing?

'I'll think about it,' said Angie.

The Atlantic Hotel, in Higher Tinworthy, was a large granite Victorian building in its own grounds, and one of several similar imposing properties in the area. Inside had been decorated in pale, ice-creamy colours, with a lot of soft, thick carpeting underfoot.

The main lounge – where tea was served – was enormous, with a row of windows looking out over the countryside towards the coast. The walls were painted a pale yellow, the carpet was a soft blue and the curtains were patterned in pink, blue and cream. A fire blazed in the white-painted fireplace at the far end. It was a pastel paradise of sweet-pea colours that Kate never for one moment would have associated with Sandra Miller. And the place was completely empty.

Kate sat down on a pink chair, and Angie sat on a blue one, to await the arrival of the tea on the white table. The young waitress arrived with an enormous plate of assorted dainty sandwiches and a cake stand groaning with scones and cakes, all accompanied by pretty dishes of butter, jams and clotted cream.

'My God,' said Angie, 'we certainly won't want any dinner tonight.'

'How come we're the only customers?' Kate asked the waitress.

'The guests are all out on a bus tour,' said the waitress. 'And Marianne's – down by the beach – do afternoon tea at half the price.'

'Have you worked here long?' Kate asked.

'About a year,' the girl replied.

'What's Mrs Miller like to work for?' Kate asked casually.

'All right.'

'Is she a good boss? Fair?' Kate persisted, ignoring Angie's kick under the table.

'Yeah, she's OK.' The waitress hovered uncertainly.

'I hear she's got quite a temper,' Kate went on, 'even violent at times. I imagine you have to tread carefully?'

The girl cleared her throat. 'Will that be all?'

'Is Mrs Miller around?' Kate asked.

The waitress hesitated. 'I think she's working in the kitchen.'

'Do tell her Kate and Angie are here. I'm sure she'll remember us from a recent pub quiz and we'd love to have a chat.'

'What are you playing at?' Angie asked, picking up a smoked salmon sandwich as the door closed behind the waitress. 'I don't know why you're doing this; you know what a bad-tempered old boot she is.'

Two minutes later the door opened again and in walked a frowning Sandra Miller, wearing a large plastic apron and bright pink gloves. *Latex free*, Kate thought approvingly, recognising the brand. Sandra tugged at the halter and waist straps of the apron, which snapped with a loud crack, then angrily balled it up into her right hand. She then peeled off that glove so it completely encased the apron, passed it all to her left hand and pulled the left glove over it, making a neat little package. Kate had done the same things herself a thousand times when she'd been doing dressings on the ward.

'You wanted to see me?'

'Oh, Sandra,' Kate said, dabbing her mouth daintily with a large pink napkin, and realising she hadn't thought of anything sensible to say, 'I just wanted to compliment you on the beautiful décor. So pretty.'

Angie choked on a crumb and had to quickly gulp some tea.

'Some overpaid so-called interior designer came a few years back and we were stupid enough to give her free rein,' said Sandra. 'I think it's bloody awful.'

'It's very restful,' Kate said, 'and I'm sure your guests love it.'

Sandra shrugged. 'So why did you *really* want to see me?'

Kate swallowed the remains of her cucumber sandwich hastily. 'Well, just to say hello.'

'*Hello* then,' said Sandra, looking from one to the other. '*Nice to see you*. Now, why were you asking young Sharon all those questions about me?' She stared hard at Kate.

'Oh, we were just interested in you and your hotel,' Kate said.

'Why would you be interested in *me*?' Sandra continued glaring at her.

'Kate was wondering if you knew about Billy what's-his-name confessing to the murders,' Angie piped up.

Sandra's eyes narrowed. 'Everyone for miles around knows that the bastard's been arrested.' She turned her attention back to Kate. 'And rumour has it that you're very pally with Maureen Grey.'

'Only because I like her and feel sorry for her,' Kate replied, wondering where this conversation was leading.

'She's the wife of a killer who very likely helped him to do the killing,' Sandra said. 'You should be pickier about the company you keep.'

'I'm not altogether convinced that Billy Grey *is* the killer,' Kate said, feeling annoyed and thinking she might as well throw the cat in among the pigeons.

'He's *confessed*, for God's sake!' Sandra exclaimed.

'I'm still not convinced he did it,' Kate said.

'So who do you think did it then?'

'I don't know,' Kate admitted.

'I was a suspect,' Sandra said, 'so is *that* why you're here?'

'Don't be ridiculous!' Kate didn't like the way Sandra was continuing to glare at her.

'It's not at all ridiculous. I'm still not allowed to leave the area so, technically, I'm not off the hook yet. And neither is your precious Maureen, or Seymour Barker-Jones, or Dr Dickie.'

'It's just that Kate's fascinated by crime,' Angie piped up apologetically. 'Watches too much of that sort of stuff on TV.'

Sandra narrowed her eyes. 'And that *is* why you're here,' she said to Kate, 'because you can get a perfectly good afternoon tea down at Lower Tinworthy, right on your doorstep, at half the price.' She squared her shoulders and folded her arms across her bust. 'Sue said you were interested in finding the killer. Well, you can get off *my* back, madam. And pay at reception as you go out.' And with that she swept out the room.

Angie broke the short silence. 'So, that went well, didn't it?'

'Don't be sarcastic!' Kate snapped. 'And it all started to go wrong when *you* said I was fascinated by crime. Why the hell did you have to say that?'

'Because you *are*. Anyway, it got her going and from the way she reacted I definitely wouldn't be removing her from your list just yet.'

'You wouldn't?'

'I wouldn't,' Angie confirmed. She withdrew a plastic carrier from the depths of her shoulder bag and pointed at the platefuls of cakes and scones. 'What I *am* going to do is take this lot home with us, and then let's pay and get out of here.' She placed everything in layers in the bag.

As they left the hotel they saw a busload of elderly people pull up outside, and heard Sandra say sweetly, 'Welcome back! Have you had a *lovely* day?'

18

It was shortly after Kate got home from work on Tuesday that the woman arrived at her door. She'd just sat down with a cup of tea when she heard the doorbell. Immediately Barney went into paroxysms of barking. Glancing out of the side window she decided there was something vaguely familiar about the small dark woman on the doorstep. 'Shut up, Barney,' she said to the excited dog, then padded to the door in her stockinged feet.

'Are you Kate Palmer?' the woman asked.

Kate reckoned she'd definitely seen this woman somewhere before. Was she press or something?

'Yes,' Kate said warily.

'I'm Jess Davey,' said the woman and then Kate remembered seeing her in the pub with Kevin. She noticed the circle of Celtic tattoos round her wrist, which appeared to continue up her arm, disappearing under the sleeve of her red fleece. Jess Davey! What on earth…?

'I'm sorry to bother you, but it were you that found Kevin's body, weren't it?' she asked.

'Yes, it was,' Kate replied.

Jess stood silently for a moment. She avoided Kate's eye and glanced around nervously as if to check that no one was watching her.

'Do you want to come in?' Kate asked, aware that this could be her only opportunity to get to know another of the suspects on The List.

'Yeah, thanks.'

Kate led the way into the kitchen. 'How can I help you?'

'I was just wonderin',' Jess Davey replied hesitantly, 'how he was? How he looked... you know?' Her voice tailed off and Kate could see tears in her big dark eyes.

Kate thought it best to deflect this question with another. 'Would you like a cup of tea?' she asked.

'Yeah, thanks, that would be good.'

Kate boiled up the kettle again. 'You were Kevin's friend, weren't you?'

'Yeah,' Jess said sadly. 'And he weren't no killer. Just cos he took the rap for killin' that kid. He should've killed bloody Fenella years ago, but he didn't.' She sat down at the kitchen table as if exhausted by her little outburst.

'I reckon it was Seymour Barker-Jones wot killed her, cos Kevin was meeting him in the pub and you know what men are – in and out every five minutes for a fag or a pee? Seymour could easily have popped out for a minute or two.'

Jess seemed agitated so Kate thought it best to keep things as calm as possible. 'Milk? Sugar?' she asked as she fished the teabag out of the mug.

'No milk, two sugars, please.' Jess stroked Barney's head. 'Nice dog.'

'Yes, he is a nice dog. Here you are, Jess.' Kate placed the mug in front of her and sat down opposite, pushing across a box of biscuits.

'Oh thanks,' said Jess, taking two chocolate ones. She sipped her tea and munched steadily for a minute, then said, 'Did he look like he'd suffered? I mean, they say he got bashed on the head and that's what killed him.'

'I know no more about that than you do,' Kate replied. 'And yes, there was a nasty wound on the side of his head. But he looked quite peaceful.'

'Thank God for that. So why was he in the water?'

Kate shrugged. 'I really don't know.'

'Seems funny cos Kev didn't like water much,' Jess remarked.

'Well, he didn't exactly choose to go in for a swim, Jess.'

Jess took another sip. 'Bleedin' police have been all through my place.'

'Maybe they thought they'd find a clue as to who killed him?' Kate suggested.

'Well, we *know* now who killed him, because Billy Grey's confessed, hasn't he?'

'Do you think it was Billy, Jess?'

Jess shrugged. 'I dunno. Like I say, I think it was that Seymour and that's why the police was lookin' for Kev's phone.'

'The police were looking for his phone?' Kate asked.

'Yes, they was, and they found it.' Jess sniffed. 'See, Kev recorded everything Fenella said, so now the cops know that it was Fenella Barker-Jones what killed that kid. And that's why they thought Kev killed her, cos she didn't want to give him the money she'd promised.'

Kate didn't comment because she was none too sure if she was supposed to know about this or not.

'We planned a new life with that dosh,' Jess went on after a moment, her face a picture of utter misery. 'We'd have got out of Tinworthy and bought a nice little place down in Spain. In Marbella, maybe. We went there for a holiday once. Yeah, Marbella.'

'So your dreams won't come true now…' Kate could understand that Jess was devastated but couldn't condone such a move when the money came from ill-gotten means.

'Yeah, and it don't matter to them Greys that Fenella was drivin' and not Kev. They still killed him.'

'*Both* the Greys?'

'Yeah, both the Greys. He disappears for years on end and then – the moment Kev gets out – back comes Billy Grey, bastard that he is. Have you seen him?'

'No,' Kate admitted, 'I haven't had that pleasure.'

'Anyway, we know now it was him. And *she* probably helped him.' Jess took another gulp of tea and started on a second chocolate biscuit. Her appetite didn't appear to be affected by her angst.

'I should never have let him out the door Saturday night,' she went on. 'He fancied goin' along to The Tinners for a pint, but I was knackered cos I'd been workin' all day. So I says to him, "You go, Kev, and I'll just put me feet up in front of the telly." To be honest I wanted to watch *Love Island* and he didn't go much for that. And then I went to bed but I didn't worry cos I knew he'd probably got in with a crowd of his mates and they'd be celebratin' him bein' home or somethin' and they'd be drinkin' late. I were a bit worried when he weren't around in the mornin' but then I thought he'd be sleepin' it off somewhere so I went over to me mum's for Sunday dinner.'

'He didn't phone you?'

'No, cos he didn't have his phone on him cos he'd locked it away safe, see. Then you found him on Sunday evenin'. He'd left the pub late but he never got home.'

'I guess you knew him for a long time?' Kate was intrigued and determined to find out more.

'Since school,' Jess replied through a mouthful of biscuit. 'I always fancied him.' She swallowed. 'Neither of us was the brain of Britain, but we got by. Know what I mean?'

Kate nodded.

'It all went wrong when he went to work for that bloody Fenella,' Jess went on. 'Did you ever meet the cow?'

'No,' Kate replied, thinking it best not to say 'only when she was dead'.

'She'd got more blokes than you've had hot dinners,' Jess said. 'She were one of them women that was needin' sex every five minutes. She weren't bad-lookin', I suppose, but her was *old*! Must've been about sixty but that didn't stop her, did it? You'd think the old cow would have dried up by then, wouldn't you?'

Dried up at sixty? Kate decided not to comment.

'She'd got plenty money though. Went all the way to Exeter every week to get her bleedin' hair done. Dyed, of course, and I'm bloody sure she had them what's-it injections in her face, not that you'd notice cos she didn't smile much. Maybe she *couldn't* smile much, ha! She sure knew how to perform though.'

'And you knew all along that it was her – not Kevin – who was driving that day?'

''Course I did! We reckoned it might be worth a few years in the nick to get some decent money at the end of it. Five hundred thousand quid she promised him. We could've bought a bleedin' *palace* down in Spain for that money!' She paused. 'Thing is, we never thought he'd get such a long sentence. We thought maybe he'd get seven years and be out in three or four. We heard later that the judge had lost his grandson in a hit-and-run accident and was handing out sentences like bloody sweeties.'

'Why did Kevin go to work for her in the first place?' Kate asked, wishing she could record this conversation herself. She'd try to remember as much of what Jess said as she could.

'Why? Cos she was offerin' good money, that's why. Only trouble was her wantin' him to live in, and I didn't want him doin' that.'

'Couldn't you have lived up there with him?'

'Not bloody likely. Didn't like her and don't like that place. Anyway, I'd just been given a nice flat by the council and I wasn't about to be leavin' that. So he said he'd try it for a few months, did Kevin. See how it goes, was what he said.'

'So Kevin was her chauffeur?'

'He ended up bein' the chauffeur, gardener, handyman, you name it. She got her money's worth, I can tell you. And that's not *all*.' Here Jess pursed her lips and took a deep breath. 'But I ain't sayin' no more.'

'More tea?' asked Kate.

'No, I'd best be goin'. I do a bit of cleanin' at The Gull and down at The Locker Café. Just thought I'd ask about Kev… you know?'

'I know,' Kate said.

'And now at least everyone knows that neither Kevin or me killed Fenella Barker-Jones,' Jess said as she stood up. 'I'd bloody felt like it often enough but I never killed nobody.'

In spite of the double negative Kate believed her. 'Well, any time you want to pop in,' she said, 'I'm usually home by four. And I'm a good listener.'

Jess sniffed. 'Yeah, thanks, I might do that. And you can tell that bleedin' detective friend of yours that if I was goin' to kill the bitch I'd have done it bloody years ago.'

Kate was astounded. How on earth did Jess know about her friendship with Woody?

'What do you mean – "that detective friend of mine"?' she stuttered after a moment.

As she reached the door Jess said, 'There ain't much goes on round here without the whole village knowin'. Thanks for the tea and that. See yuh!'

With that she mounted her bicycle, which had been leaning against the wall, and was gone.

Kate badly wanted to speak to Woody about Jess Davey landing on her doorstep. She felt deeply sorry for Jess, who'd lost not only her partner but also her long-held dreams of a life in the sun with no money worries. That dream must have kept both her and Kevin going through the long dark years of his imprisonment. What sort of woman was Fenella Barker-Jones who would promise that money to save her own skin and then refuse to deliver? Until now she'd been inclined to feel sorry for Fenella, who'd been vilified by everyone, but now she wasn't so sure. Perhaps she couldn't help having a voracious appetite for sex, but breaking a promise of *this* magnitude…?

Why did Kate ever think she could solve this – believing herself to be some sort of Miss Marple – but getting absolutely nowhere? Why had she ever thought that, by getting to know them one by one, she'd be able to eliminate them one by one as well? Now she was sorely tempted to remove both Maureen and Jess from The List.

She was tempted, but she didn't.

Kate walked up the garden to discuss her thoughts with Angie, who had locked herself in the studio, minus the saucepan. She was furiously churning out more canvases. Far from Kate being able to discuss what was uppermost in her mind, it was Luke this and Luke that, and what name should Angie give to her latest creation? Atlantic Sunset, perhaps?

Angie was keen for Kate to know that Indian Summer was displayed inside the gallery, and was determined that Kate should go to see how clever Luke was for positioning it just right and lighting it to its best advantage.

'Presentation is the name of the game, Luke says,' Angie explained. 'Why don't you come and see?'

As they walked down to the gallery Angie told Kate that Luke was expecting Lower Tinworthy to be swamped by tourists from now on, the more discerning of whom would be only too happy to part with two hundred and fifty pounds for the privilege of hanging Indian Summer on their walls.

'*Two hundred and fifty pounds!*' Kate stared at her sister in disbelief. 'Are you kidding?'

When she arrived at The Gallery and saw Angie's painting, Kate had to admit that Angie's red and gold splashes of paint did look better when artfully displayed.

'You look surprised,' Luke said as he emerged from the workshop at the rear. He was clad in tight jeans and a black sweatshirt opened

– artfully, of course – halfway down his chest to expose a chunky gold chain. His blond locks were carefully swept to one side and Kate suspected he was wearing mascara. *No*, she thought, *I don't think I need to worry too much about him and Angie.*

'I *am* surprised,' she said, staring at the picture and trying to decipher any sort of design. She looked around the gallery at the variety of paintings on display and could only imagine a couple of them on her wall. There was, however, some locally crafted silver jewellery that she did like and some overpriced chunky pottery.

'You won't see much of me from now on ,' Angie announced cheerfully. In honour of the occasion she'd tied her hair up into a messy topknot and was wearing a paint-splashed smock over her jeans. Every inch the artist.

But Kate was pleased. Angie had come alive and, even better, appeared to be spending less time at the pub.

And there was always the possibility, she supposed, that somebody might even buy Indian Summer.

19

Some things are meant to happen, Kate decided. She had a day off on the Thursday and decided it was time for a visit to Truro to buy some curtain material for her bedroom to complement her newly painted walls. The window latch still didn't close properly and she planned to find someone to fix it before next winter as she didn't fancy a cold draught now that her bed was directly in front of it.

'Do you fancy a trip to Truro?' Kate asked Angie.

Angie didn't; it was becoming busy at The Gallery and wouldn't it be awful if someone were to buy her painting and she *wasn't there*?

Kate set off on her own and was halfway down the A39 when her mobile rang. She could see a layby a short distance ahead and prayed she'd get there before the caller rang off. It might just be Maureen.

'Hi!' There was that unmistakeable American accent again. 'Woody here. I'm sorry to bother you but I wondered if you might do me a favour?'

'Yes, of course,' Kate replied.

'I've got a feeling that I've left my kitchen window wide open and I wondered if – and *only* if – you might be walking the dog up to the coastal path today whether you might pop by and just push it shut? Thing is, I'm at a meeting in Truro and won't be back until the evening.'

Truro! Kate took a deep breath. 'Believe it or not, Woody, I'm on my way to Truro right now.'

'You are?'

'Shall I call my sister and ask her to close the window?'

'No, don't worry about it – it's at the back of the house anyway so probably OK. What are you up to in Truro?'

'Just hunting for some curtain fabric.'

'Look, I've got meetings here all day but I'm free between twelve and two. How do you fancy some lunch?'

'That would be lovely,' Kate said with feeling.

'How about we meet up at The Tarry Inn. Do you know it?'

Kate didn't, so he gave her detailed directions. 'It's not too far to walk from Lemon Quay but it's sufficiently out of the way that we're not likely to run into half of Tinworthy.'

'That's great,' Kate said, frantically scribbling with an eyebrow pencil on a crumpled-up receipt and vowing never to leave home without a pen again. 'What time?'

'Quarter after twelve all right for you?'

'Absolutely,' Kate said. She was unable to stop smiling as she pulled out of the layby.

The Tarry Inn was an ancient timber-framed building with low ceilings, black beams and woodwork, and old leaded-light windows. Kate wondered if it was Elizabethan. It was also renowned for its pies.

Woody was waiting at the bar clutching a half pint of lager. His face lit up when Kate arrived. 'Hey,' he said, 'isn't this some coincidence!' And he kissed her on the cheek. 'I couldn't believe it when you said you were coming here. What'll you have?'

'A white wine spritzer would be lovely,' Kate said. 'How was your daughter and your trip to London?'

'The daughter is just fine but I was glad to get away from London and the crowds. It seems to be busier than ever up there, but maybe that's because I've become acclimatised to Cornwall.'

They carried their drinks to a corner table and sat down to study the vast array of pies that were available: steak and kidney; steak and ale; salmon and haddock; chicken and ham; potato and leek; cheese and onion. She told Woody that she'd seen some attractive blue-and-cream fabric that she thought would be suitable and Woody told her about the CID meeting, and about how he'd made an excuse not to join the others for lunchtime beers. It was only small talk but it felt special.

'They probably think I'm antisocial,' he said, 'but I'd much rather spend the time with you.' He smiled.

Kate was completely disarmed for a moment and could only say, 'Thank you.'

'You realise,' he said, 'that we still shouldn't really be seen together because you're a witness. But now that there's the possibility we have our killer we should soon be able to rectify that.'

'You don't sound too sure,' Kate said.

'I'm not convinced that Billy Grey *is* our man,' he said. 'But we have narrowed it down considerably, although you'll realise that I can't really give out that information to anyone, not even you. There's a lot going on behind the scenes and I'm hoping for another arrest before too long but, for God's sake, don't repeat that to anyone.'

'I promise I won't,' Kate said and decided it was time to tell him what Maureen had said. 'And I think you're right to be doubtful because Maureen thinks he confessed purely so she would be off the hook. He seems to have suddenly developed a conscience about leaving her for ten years and setting up home with someone else, incredible though that may seem after all this time.'

'In this job,' Woody said, studying the menu, 'nothing surprises me anymore. All the time he was away he was paying her an allowance. Did she tell you that?'

'No.'

'What I don't understand is why she's apparently never questioned it. If your husband disappeared but continued to pay you an allowance, you'd probably want to trace him and where the money was coming from, wouldn't you?'

'I certainly would,' Kate agreed. She paused. 'I've met Sandra Miller a couple of times recently; strange woman.'

'Ah, Sandra Miller,' he repeated slowly. 'Yeah, she's known to be a bit fiery. She was a suspect for Fenella's murder at first but Kevin Barry gave her an alibi. He saw her outside the WI when he went out for a smoke and went over to speak to her. And the landlord at The Tinners saw them both out there together. I don't much like the woman but I don't think she's a killer.'

Perhaps I should remove her from my list, Kate thought. *Perhaps I should tear the whole list up.*

'But not impossible,' he added.

I won't tear it up, she decided. 'I'm working on my other suspects.'

'Your other suspects? Are you seriously investigating, Kate? And who might the other suspects be?'

'Well, I've become quite friendly with Seymour Barker-Jones,' Kate said.

'How did you manage that?'

'There's a great advantage in having a dog, you know. You frequently chat to anyone else you meet with a dog. And Seymour walks his up on the cliffs same as I do.'

'So he comes all the way down from Higher T to walk his dogs on the coastal path? I'd have thought there were plenty of walks up on the moors where he lives. Wonder why he goes there?'

'Perhaps he likes the sea. He seems to like sitting on that seat up there and looking out at the Atlantic. He told me he once sat on the seat with Fenella. He also hinted that he was "unable to fulfil all her requirements", or words to that effect.'

'He told you that?'

Kate could see that she'd surprised Woody. 'Yes, he seemed very sad.'

'Hmmm,' said Woody. 'Let's eat.'

Kate ordered a fish pie while Woody settled for steak and ale.

'Everyone wants this thing tied up,' he said, as they waited for their food. 'Not least your friend Seymour, who's badgering me about when he can go back to London, but until we have proof that Billy Grey did this I can't really allow any of the suspects to leave the area.'

'So Seymour's still a suspect?'

'Technically yes, although he does supposedly have an alibi in that Mrs Tilley, his housekeeper, swears he was back there at the time of the murder. Mind you, she's known to play Radio Cornwall all day long at full volume, so he could have gone out, met Kevin at The Tinners for a drink and come back again and she'd be none the wiser.'

'I've met Mrs Tilley,' Kate said. 'She was keen to tell me about the police coming to the door and Seymour crying out like a banshee, she said. All this excitement caused her to slice her forefinger with the knife she was using to cut vegetables.'

'There's a lot of sharp knives around,' Woody said with a wicked grin.

'That's what Mrs Tilley said. Anyway, I'm going to hang on to my list of the suspects and I'm going to try to see them all and hopefully find some clues.'

The pies arrived.

'These look wonderful,' Woody said, 'and I'm starving!'

They ate in silence for a minute before Woody said, 'How's your pie?'

'Absolutely delicious! But getting back to my list, there's Dr Payne, of course.'

'Yes, you're right,' Woody said, smiling. 'Dr Dickie can't be ruled out. Neighbours saw him leave the house in his car that evening and come back about forty minutes later. He says he drove to the supermarket because they'd run out of milk, but saw no one he knew. He doesn't appear on any of the closed-circuit cameras. He went *somewhere* though.'

'I went up to their house,' Kate said.

'You did? Why?'

'Part of my community nursing duties, to see Mrs Payne. I thought he was a bit peculiar but he looked harmless enough. And Mrs Payne is a great deal more clued-up than everyone makes her out to be. I got the impression that she knows exactly what's going on.'

He looked thoughtful. 'That's interesting. I only met her briefly when she confirmed that they had run out of milk that evening.'

'This is where I have an advantage,' Kate said. '*You* can't get close to them but *I* can. And don't forget that I have to make a list of patients' problems and symptoms and then try to work out what might be causing them, so I'm used to doing a bit of detective work.'

'Yes, I guess you are.' He looked a little worried. 'You should leave the detective work to us though, Kate. Who else is on your list?'

'Well, apart from the serial killer that Angie is convinced is lying in wait, there's Jess Davey.'

'I think we can count the serial killer out,' Woody said, 'with apologies to Angie.'

'I had a visit from Jess Davey.'

Woody stopped chewing. 'You did? Why did she come to see you?'

'She wanted to know if Kevin looked peaceful when I found him on the beach. Then she went on about Fenella not paying up and how all their dreams had been shattered,' Kate said.

'Their dreams?'

Kate laid down her knife and fork. 'Yes, apparently they were planning to get away and buy a place in Spain.'

Woody shook his head. 'Well, I suppose poor Kevin reckoned he'd earned his house in Spain if he spent seven years in jail for something he didn't do. So nobody could blame Jess if she stuck the knife in Fenella, but that doesn't solve Kevin's murder. I'm amazed she came to see you. Why did she?'

'I think it's because I'm a nurse – people are happy to chat, not just about their health, but anything else that comes into their heads. A bit like people chat a lot to their hairdressers. And that way I'm hoping to get to know all the suspects and that maybe one of them will drop their guard.'

'Kate,' Woody said, leaning forward and looking into her eyes, '*please* be careful. You could be walking on dangerous ground if one of them is guilty. And that, of course, is one of the main reasons why no one must know we're friends, because if they thought you were extracting information and passing it on to me…'

'No one knows,' Kate said more confidently than she felt after Jess Davey's remark.

'Well, your sister knows,' Woody reminded her. 'And Maureen may have guessed.'

'Angie won't tell,' Kate said, trying to keep the doubt out of her voice and aware that Luke probably knew. 'Anyway, if you're not one hundred per cent convinced by Billy Grey's confession, then why aren't you still investigating the others?'

'Because,' Woody replied, 'now we have someone in custody I can't waste police time and resources. But, like I say, this is police work. Just be very careful and take no chances. Whatever you do, don't be alone with any of them, because there's a real chance that our killer is still out there. I know you mean well,' he said gently, 'but if someone suspects you're probing there could be dire consequences, particularly if it's one person who's killed twice. You must *not* become number three.' He drained his glass. 'I'm serious, Kate. Don't get too close to any of them, not even Maureen. And

Sandra Miller would be quite fit to thump you at the very least!'
There was a glimmer of a smile on his face. He glanced at his watch.
'We still have half an hour, so no more shop talk. Tell me about
yourself and your sons, Kate. Has there been anyone else since your
divorce all those years ago?'

'I've had a few relationships,' Kate admitted, remembering the
builder who'd shared her life for five years and built her an amazing
conservatory. And the head teacher who'd asked her out after she'd
visited the school for parents' day, a relationship which lasted for
four years, much to the horror of her boys. 'They were beyond
being embarrassed at their mother going out with "Old Mac", so
called because his name was MacKay and he was all of forty-six.
Then I met a few on an online dating agency, including an actor
who used to ask me to listen to him trying to memorise his lines.
To this day I can recite a fair amount of *King Lear*!'

Woody laughed. 'Well, I've met a few ladies since my wife
died. I was surprised at how many policewomen decided I needed
looking after and I have to say they cooked me some great meals.'

Kate could believe that – he really was very fanciable indeed.

'There was one who lasted a few years,' he went on, 'but she
wasn't a policewoman, she was a physiotherapist. I had some muscle
injuries after playing rugby and I was sent to be manipulated by
Kerry. And boy, did she manipulate me!'

Kate felt an irrational surge of anger towards the manipulative
Kerry.

He reached across and took her hand in his. 'And now there's
you! Though I'm just sorry we can't spend more time together at
the moment,' he said, still holding her hand. 'I have to leave shortly
but I'll be in touch as soon as I can. Hopefully we can lunch closer
to home in the not-too-distant future.'

He insisted on paying for the meals and then, outside on the
pavement, he gave her a quick hug and said, 'Take care, Kate.'

20

'Your turn to visit Clare Payne,' Sue said when Kate arrived at the surgery the following morning.

Kate had been wondering how to contrive a meeting with Dickie Payne again. More importantly she wondered how to get him on his own and hopefully find out something about the man. Sue had given her an opportunity.

'Did you know that Dr Dickie has one of the largest collection of medical instruments in the country?' Sue went on. 'You'd find it fascinating, if a bit creepy. Some of the scalpels and things go back centuries.'

'How interesting,' murmured Kate. 'I'd love to see it.'

'Well, just ask him. He's very proud of it, particularly as the BBC came down to film it a year or so ago.'

As Kate drove up to Higher Tinworthy she realised this could be her one and only chance to have a chat with the old doctor. And, as a nurse, she had every reason to be fascinated by his collection of medical instruments, creepy or not. *Please be at home*, she prayed.

There was no sign of Dickie when she arrived. The door was opened by a tiny lady in a floral pinny brandishing a feather duster. 'Come in,' she said, leading the way through the hallway into the sitting room. 'Mrs Payne will be with you in a minute.'

Kate looked around; no sign of Dickie. Just her luck.

'How nice to see you again!' Clare exclaimed as she propelled herself into the room.

'Hello,' said Kate. 'How are you?'

'Not so bad,' Clare said. Then, shouting: '*Mabel!* Can you bring us both a cup of tea?'

Mabel mumbled something vaguely affirmative from the hallway.

While Kate attended to the leg she asked casually, 'Where's the doctor today?'

'Oh, he's around somewhere,' Clare said. 'He's not too happy because he wanted to go to a retired doctors' conference in Bristol, which would have necessitated him having to stay up there over-night, and the police have forbidden him to go. I don't understand it at all, particularly as they now have a self-confessed murderer in custody.'

'It does seem strange,' Kate agreed.

'What *more* do they want?' Kate could hear the agitation in Clare's voice. 'They have someone in custody who's admitted to the murders; surely it couldn't be simpler?'

'You'd think so, wouldn't you?' Kate concurred. 'And I can't think why they suspected your husband in the first place. It seems incredible to me. Just because he was out for a little while at the time of Fenella's murder.' She wondered for a moment if she'd gone too far.

'Hopefully they'll find the cashier who served him.' Clare sighed. 'You haven't been here very long, have you, my dear? Dickie was very friendly with Fenella, you know. Very friendly. They'd been friends for years and years. But she was a demanding woman and she and Dickie fell out. That's the crux of it. Something quite trivial, I believe. They'd fallen out and *everyone* knew about it.'

Kate wasn't sure what to say next. 'He chose a bad time to go for the milk,' she said after a minute. 'But why did neither he nor his car appear on the closed-circuit televisions at the supermarket?'

'How do you know *that*?' Clare asked shortly.

Kate hesitated. She'd better tread carefully. 'I heard it somewhere,' she said.

'I would say that the fault stems from a non-operating camera, not from Dickie,' she said firmly. 'These things don't pick up *everyone*, you know.'

'I'm sure you're right,' Kate said hastily. 'It's just that I find the case fascinating and I like to get everyone's angle on it.'

At this point Mabel appeared with a tray with the tea things on it, and a small plate of biscuits. Kate sipped for a moment.

'Well, my dear,' Clare continued, 'I should be concentrating on the Greys if I were you. He came back from wherever he'd been specifically to commit these awful crimes and I've no doubt whatsoever that she assisted him. Let's face it, they never got losing their child, so one can have some sympathy I suppose.'

'Oh, indeed,' Kate murmured as she finished bandaging.

'Not that I've had children myself,' Clare said, 'that wasn't to be. But I can imagine how dreadful it must be to lose a child. Dreadful.'

'That's your leg done,' Kate said as she began to pack everything away. 'I'm disappointed not to see the doctor though; I understand he has a very impressive collection of medical instruments?'

'Oh, he's around somewhere,' Clare said and, as if on cue, the door opened and in walked Dickie.

'Ah,' he said as Kate drained her tea, 'it's our new nurse again.'

'Yes,' Clare said, 'and she'd like to see your collection, darling.'

'If it's not too much trouble,' Kate put in.

'Oh, it's no trouble at all, my dear,' said Dr Dickie. 'If you've finished here then do come with me.'

Kate got to her feet, set her empty cup down on the tray and said goodbye to Clare, before following him out of the room and down a long corridor with a threadbare dark green carpet at the back of the house. The grey-painted walls were adorned with graphic anatomical diagrams: bones, muscles, veins and arteries. Kate felt as if she was walking through one of the textbooks from her student nursing days. He stopped at the far end, withdrew a key from his pocket, unlocked a door and ushered her into an enormous room, shelved from floor to ceiling, with tables in the centre, and every surface jammed full of labelled exhibits. There was an array of instruments such as scalpels, syringes, forceps, clamps, stethoscopes, jars and cases with weird contents, among them a pickled appendix in a glass container, and there was even an iron lung positioned at the far end of the room. There was also a display of surgeons' gowns, masks and gloves.

'Some of these instruments go back hundreds of years,' Dickie said proudly.

As she looked around it seemed to Kate to be more out of a horror film than anything else. She moved quickly away from a thumb in a glass jar, her appetite for lunch destroyed. She shuddered.

He noticed. 'I wouldn't have thought a nurse would be squeamish,' he said.

'I'm just not too keen on seeing body parts on display,' Kate said, 'particularly if they've been around for a hundred years.'

'Oh, really?' he said. Then, turning to her: 'I understand from what you've been saying to my wife that you think I'm connected to these murders in some way.'

'Of course not!' Kate said hastily. 'I only said—'

'I know what you said,' he interrupted. 'I was listening at the door. You seemed to find my trip to the supermarket of great interest.'

'No, no, I was only repeating what someone said.' Kate began to edge her way back towards the door, moving more quickly past a collection of gleaming scalpels.

'And who might that someone be?' he asked.

'I really can't remember now. I see so many people in the course of the day.'

'You shouldn't believe everything you hear,' he said.

Was it her imagination or did he sound menacing? 'You're quite right,' she said as she got to the door. 'Thank you for showing me your impressive collection. It's been most interesting, but I must be on my way now.'

'Indeed you must,' he said, locking the door behind him as they emerged into the corridor. 'You're a practice nurse so I know you must be a very busy woman.' He then accompanied her to the front door, looked up at the sky, and said, 'Looks like rain.'

'Yes it does,' she agreed, relieved to be out in the open air. He stood on the step and watched her as she got into her car.

It was with some relief that Kate put the car into gear and drove away. Murderer or not, there was something very unsettling about the man.

When she got home she found a rolled-up newspaper addressed to her. It was a copy of the *Cornish Courier*, and on page four was an article written by Jordan Jarvis and a not-very-flattering photograph of Kate looking like a startled rabbit caught in the headlights.

'*Nurse Kate Palmer,*' he'd written, '*was walking along the beach at Lower Tinworthy with her dog when she spied what she thought was a large bundle of something washed up by the tide. This turned out to be the body of Kevin Barry, who was the main suspect in the murder of Mrs Fenella Barker-Jones of Higher Tinworthy. Billy Grey, who recently returned to the village from London, has now admitted to both crimes. Mrs Palmer must wonder why she left city crime behind to seek peaceful retirement in an, until now, sleepy Cornish village.*' It went on to say that Mrs Palmer was a mother and (almost) a grandmother, had seen plenty of knife crime in London and was most interested in getting to the bottom of this particular case. 'I'm naturally curious,' she was quoted as saying. Had she said that? Probably. She couldn't remember.

Kate didn't know how many people in Tinworthy actually bought the *Cornish Courier* but was sure it wasn't too many. She could do without this publicity at the moment.

21

After Kate got home and digested Jordan's article, she decided to do some gardening to distract herself for a while from the murders. It was a beautiful sunny April evening. The front – which overlooked the river and the sea – got more than its share of wind and salt-spray. It had been laid mainly to lawn, bordered with hydrangeas, Sea Breeze and, of course, lavender, all of which were able to withstand the vagaries of the Cornish weather. The grass needed cutting and the borders needed weeding so Kate got to work, happy to be in the fresh air. Although it was warm Kate shivered a little as she recalled Dickie Payne and his creepy medical relics. She was aware that she'd managed to annoy both him and Sandra Miller over the last few days, so she wasn't doing a brilliant job of playing an undercover super sleuth. And Woody would be annoyed; he'd told her to be careful.

She glanced across the valley at the hill opposite and saw a glint of something in the sun. Kate stood for a moment and stared. There it was again. The reflection of sunshine on glass? Could it be someone using binoculars? It was coming from somewhere above Woody's house, towards the coastal path. And someone was walking up there. Kate needed to find her own binoculars to see who it could be. She went inside and, after a search, found them in the so-called dining room, under a pile of sheets. But by the time she got outside there was no trace of anyone on the hill opposite. Kate had an uncomfortable feeling that someone had been spying, but decided that her imagination was running away with her and put it to the back of her mind. It could be *anyone* looking at *anything*, for goodness' sake!

It took a couple of hours to cut the grass and weed the front garden before she moved round to the back, which had the hill rising behind it and so got a limited amount of light. There was the garage, full of everything under the sun except a car; a shed crammed full of stuff they hadn't yet unpacked; a pear tree; a hedge of lavender and, of course, the summerhouse at the top of the slope. There was also one small flowerbed full of weeds and not much else. When they'd arrived Angie had enthusiastically suggested they grow a few vegetables there, but Angie was good on suggestions and not so good on doing anything about them. Kate wondered if she had enough energy left to dig some of it at least.

She'd dug about half of it before she gave up, exhausted, and went indoors to make a cup of tea. Then, looking at the clock, realised it was after six o'clock and she'd done nothing about dinner. Tea be damned, she thought, reaching for the bottle of Merlot. She poured herself a generous glassful and wondered if there might be something in the freezer that would be easy to cook.

Just then the phone rang. It was Angie to say that she and Luke were staying open until seven o'clock and then they were going to have a pub meal. Kate extracted a cannelloni from the freezer and stuck it in the microwave. She decided she'd be in bed by nine, ten at the latest. For a brief moment she wondered if she should phone Woody but then decided against it. There didn't seem to be much point in calling him only to inform him that she'd managed to annoy two of the remaining suspects.

Kate ate her supper, had two more glasses of wine, was in bed by nine thirty and asleep by ten.

When she woke just after six o'clock Kate was aware of two things: a cold blast of air and something fluttering alongside her face. As she slowly came round she stared in astonishment at the wide-open window, knowing that she hadn't left it like that. Granted, it didn't close properly, so perhaps there'd been gusts of wind in the night. And then she saw what was fluttering. It was a small piece of paper, which was anchored into her pillow with a very long pin. It looked like a pearl hatpin. Had Angie left her a note when she came in? Kate couldn't imagine she'd have done it this way and, besides, Angie certainly didn't have a hatpin.

Rubbing her eyes, Kate sat up in bed and pulled out the pin and the note, which was typed and looked as if it had been printed from a computer. *What on earth?*

And there, in a flamboyant large font, it said:

STOP MEDDLING. LEAVE WELL ALONE OR YOU'LL BE SORRY

Kate had often wondered what it felt like to have your blood run cold, and now she knew. For a moment she felt nauseous, and not just because of what was written, but by the fact that someone had come in through the window at least far enough to leave this note on her pillow while she was asleep.

They could just as easily have cut her throat.

She looked out of the window and could only suppose that the person had climbed up onto the kitchen extension roof, which was entirely possible by using the ladder that was permanently wedged between the shed and the garage. After that, she supposed, it would be easy enough to vault up onto the windowsill. And now that her bed was directly under the window he or she would only have needed to lean in to stab that pin into her pillow. How did that person know that this bedroom was hers? Had someone been watching her? Watching the windows at the back of the house? From where? Further up the hill? How often had she stood at that window in her nightie, pulling the curtains back before she got into bed because she liked the cool night air? Her mind went back to the flash of the sun on binocular lenses the day before.

Kate continued to feel sick. She would have to take the note to the police station and tell Woody what she'd been up to, because plainly she had hit a nerve somewhere with someone.

She came slowly downstairs, gulped a glass of water, put the kettle on to boil and looked at her watch. Seven o'clock. She couldn't phone Woody yet, better wait for another hour at least. Angie would be unlikely to surface before nine and so there was no one in whom she could confide or show the note to. Of course Angie would only say something like, 'Well, if you *will* get involved in things that don't concern you…' and Woody would probably say, 'I *told* you to be careful, didn't I?' He might even put some form of police protection on the house and then the whole village would judge her either to be a suspect, or a meddling busybody, or at least to have been connected with the case in some way and so put everyone on their guard. Nevertheless, with her life possibly in danger, what else could she do?

She drank her tea, switched on breakfast television and tried to care about Manchester United versus Chelsea, about the bin strike in Birmingham or about the rain approaching from the west. Rain was always approaching from the west.

And all the time Kate was staring at the note. Would there be fingerprints on it? Almost certainly not; the person would have worn gloves. Should she wait until nine o'clock? Woody probably didn't get to his office until nine so there was little point in ringing earlier.

At half past eight – just as Kate was composing what she planned to say to Woody – he phoned.

'Kate? My apologies for calling you so early.'

She loved his voice. How did he know she was planning to phone him? Did they have some sort of telepathy? This was incredible!

'Hi, Woody, I was just about to—'

'Sorry to interrupt, Kate,' he said. 'But Maureen Grey has disappeared. *Gone!* Done a runner overnight. One of our guys checked on her this morning only to be told by a neighbour that she'd gone away late last night sometime, carrying a little suitcase, and had asked this neighbour to feed the cat while she was gone. We're trying to trace where the hell she might go. You've become quite friendly with her so I wondered if you had any ideas?'

Kate didn't need to think for long. 'No, sorry,' she lied. 'But surely she's not a suspect anymore so why does it matter where she is?'

'Well, for one thing I'm not at all sure that she *isn't* a suspect because she's certainly acting like one.' Woody sighed. 'And secondly I'm not at all convinced that her husband *is* the killer. I think he might be putting up a shield to allow her to escape. This could be a plan they've cooked up between them. If you think of anything or anywhere she could be, would you contact us? Sorry, Kate, I've got a caller on the other line so I've got to go.'

Kate sat down, her heart thumping. She should, of course, have told him about the note before he hung up. She could call back but she had a feeling he would then add two and two together and come up with the answer she feared. Because who else would leave a note on her pillow and then abscond late at night? It all pointed to Maureen.

Kate tried to think logically about the suspects. Who would, or would not, be able to climb up onto the roof and heave themselves up to her bedroom window?

Seymour Barker-Jones? He looked fit enough. He was known to be in the civil service but it was an open secret in the village that he was MI5, so it wasn't beyond the bounds of imagination that such a James Bond-like stunt might appeal to him. And she'd told him about the list. She shouldn't have done that, but had it really upset him? You could never really tell.

Then there was Dickie Payne. He was old, but he was slim and seemed to be in good health, so he could probably have managed it. It was only yesterday she'd spoken to him and he'd guessed that she suspected him. And why had he been listening outside the door when she was chatting to Clare? And where had he been for that hour at the time of Fenella's murder?

What about Sandra Miller? Kate had also got on the wrong side of Sandra, but she couldn't imagine the impetuous, quick-tempered Sandra mulling it over for hours. And yet...

It couldn't be Billy Grey, now in custody through his own admission, an admission Kate didn't believe for a minute. It was obvious – as far as Kate was concerned – that he was doing it out of guilt for the way he'd treated Maureen. And that left Maureen, of course. Kate must have been the only person in Tinworthy who'd been *so* convinced that Maureen was innocent. And it stood to reason that, if she *had* delivered that note, she'd probably have been on her way somewhere. Now Kate was full of doubt. One thing was for certain though: she *had* to find Maureen. She had to find her before the police did, to give her a chance to explain or to prove her innocence in some way – that's *if* she was innocent.

And Kate was pretty certain she knew where to find her.

Kate tried to plan her day. She needed an excuse to pop into the medical centre on a day off but she reckoned it would be so manic in there on a Friday morning that no one would notice her. She'd say she had some paperwork to catch up on.

Angie had surfaced. 'Morning,' she said as she tottered in the door. 'Is the kettle hot?'

Kate flicked the switch. 'Good morning.' She was thinking quickly. She decided she wouldn't tell Angie about the note because she was bound to tell Luke, who was an unknown quantity, or more likely, she'd panic and insist on calling the police. No, no, no; not yet.

'Angie,' she said as the kettle came to the boil, 'I'm thinking of going up to London today. Well, to Shirley's in Windsor anyway, and hopefully I'll be back tomorrow evening.'

'*What!*' Angie almost dropped her mug. 'What on earth are you going up there for?'

'I'll tell you when I get back,' Kate said.

'Tell me now, for God's sake!'

'Just something I need to check on.'

'C'mon, Kate, you'll have to do better than that. What are you up to? Don't tell me it's something to do with this list of yours?'

'Well, maybe. But I need you to be here on and off tomorrow, to look after Barney and take him for a walk. He can't be on his own all day. And, after all, he is supposed to be *your* dog. I'll give him a walk in a minute before I leave.'

Angie sipped her tea. 'I'll look after Barney tomorrow if you tell me where you're going, and why. Come on – supposing you had an accident or something?'

Kate reconsidered. 'OK then. I think Maureen's gone up there. Woody's just phoned to say she's disappeared and I think I know where she's gone.'

'Oh no, not *Maureen* again!'

'Yes, Maureen again. I think she's up there and I intend to bring her back. Now don't ask any more questions.'

'Is this the wonderful Woody's doing? Has he asked you to do this? If you tell him where you think she is then surely he could send some *police* there to get her? Why's she done a runner anyway? Don't you think that's the act of a guilty woman?'

'Believe me, it'll be easier if I go myself, Angie. I'll be back by tomorrow night.'

Angie refilled her mug. 'You're nuts. This is taking Super Sleuth Kate Palmer a bit too far! You're not Miss Bloody Marple!'

'Miss Marple or not, I'm going.'

Angie sighed. 'OK, OK, I just hope you know what you're doing.'

'And please don't tell Luke, or anyone, where I'm going. *Please!*'

'OK, OK!'

'Just one more thing, Angie. My window blew open sometime during the night; there must have been a gust of wind or something; it was cold and draughty when I woke up – so would you be kind enough to contact that locksmith next to the post office and ask him to come as soon as possible to replace the catch and install a lock of some kind? Monday, hopefully?'

'It wasn't windy last night. Wonder why it blew open?'

'No idea. But would you do that, please?'

Kate drained her tea, made a quick phone call to her friend Shirley in Windsor and then dashed upstairs to pack an overnight bag before taking Barney for a half-hour walk.

She planned to be on her way by late morning.

22

As expected, the surgery was frantically busy. There was a queue of people at the reception desk and as Kate slipped in behind she called out to Denise, 'Something I need to write up in my notes, I'll just pop in and get them.' Denise nodded, waved and carried on dealing with the queue.

Kate headed for the filing cabinets. G for Grey; not Billy, not Maureen. Ah, *Janet* Grey, aged seventy-two, who lived at Highfield Cottage, Higher Tinworthy. That would be her.

Mission successful. Kate closed the drawer, scribbled the address on a scrap of paper and waved to Denise, giving her a thumbs up, on the way out. 'Saw the article in the *Courier*,' Denise yelled. 'Not a very flattering photo though!'

Kate nodded, cursed Jordan and the photo, then got into her car and headed up to Higher Tinworthy, passing Pendorian Manor, the Paynes' and The Atlantic Hotel, as well as all the other smart addresses, before the road dipped down to where there was a straggling row of smaller houses.

Highfield Cottage was at the far end of the lane. It was tiny, painted white at some time in the distant past, with windows that had once been painted red, most of which had now peeled off. The front garden was neat and tidy though and half of it had been dug into a vegetable patch. Mrs Grey obviously preferred gardening to painting.

Kate took a deep breath and knocked on the door, praying that the woman would be in. A few moments later the door was opened by a small, stout woman with short grey hair, clad in tracksuit bottoms and a blue fleece top.

'Mrs Grey?'

'Who's askin'?'

'Um, well, I'm Kate Palmer and I'm a nurse at the medical centre.'

'I seen your photo in the paper. So what do you want?'

'Well, I'm here about Maureen—'

'*Maureen!* Nothing but trouble, that one! What's she done *now*?'

'She's disappeared, I'm afraid.' Kate looked around. 'Do you think I could come in?'

Mrs Grey sniffed and stood aside. 'You'd better, I suppose. Don't want her next door hearing every word, nosy old cow.'

Kate stepped into a hallway with a violently patterned carpet in reds and browns, while Mrs Grey closed the outside door and then ushered her into a tiny lounge with a different – but even more violently patterned – carpet in orange and black. There was flower-sprigged wallpaper and every surface was covered with china ladies, dogs and cats, glass birds, and half a dozen or so vases containing dusty plastic flowers.

'Sit down then,' said Mrs Grey, indicating one of the upright chintz-covered armchairs.

Kate wondered if she dared sit down without knocking some knickknack flying. She seated herself carefully and Mrs Grey sat down opposite her under a picture of a green Chinese lady.

'My Billy's in prison,' she said, 'thanks to that wife of his.'

'I'm not convinced that either Billy or Maureen had anything to do with these murders,' Kate said. 'And I've become fond of Maureen.'

'Huh!' said Mrs Grey. 'No accounting for taste. She went funny after Lucy got killed and she's still funny if you ask me. She spent time in Bodmin, you know. Went for my Billy with a bread knife, she did.'

'Yes, but that was immediately after the tragedy when she was under unbearable stress. Anyway, Mrs Grey, I want to find Maureen. She left sometime last night apparently.'

'*Guilty*, that's why. And she's left poor Billy to swing for her.' She dabbed her eyes with a rose-embroidered handkerchief.

'Well, my guess is that she's gone up to London to see the woman Billy's been living with,' Kate said. 'But I may be wrong.'

Mrs Grey's eyes widened. 'Why on God's earth would she do that?'

'Because she was particularly interested in the little girl.'

'Oh my God!' Mrs Grey clutched her throat in horror. 'She's most likely planning to kill her too! Oh *no*! I should call the police right now!'

Kate held up her hand. 'Don't do that, Mrs Grey, *please*. Let me go up there and bring Maureen back, and see if I can find some sort of proof to show that Billy didn't do this. I'm almost as keen as you are to see him set free.'

Mrs Grey stared at her while she digested this. 'Why? What's it to you?'

'Because I'm sure your son didn't do it and, in that case, the real murderer is still out there.' *And I have proof,* Kate thought. The note was safely in her shoulder bag.

'So,' she continued, 'what I really want is the address of Billy's lady in London.'

'The police could give you that,' Mrs Grey said with a snort, 'cos they've been round there a few times pokin' about and askin' questions.'

Kate decided to be honest. 'Two things,' she said, 'the first one being that I don't think the police *would* give me the address and, secondly, I don't want them to know where I'm going in case they go crashing in there first to see what's going on. The police do a lot of questioning; they like facts. They don't chat and get to know people, but I do. First and foremost, I need to find Maureen and then I need to see if I can find some sort of proof to get Billy off the hook. I don't know your son, Mrs Grey, but I don't think he's guilty.'

Mrs Grey sighed. 'They were courtin' in school, you know, Billy and Mo. Pretty little thing she was but she's let herself go since Lucy… And she blamed Billy, see? All because Billy sent her down to the letter box to post his football pool. No one was to know that Kevin Barry would come crashing along on the wrong side of the road.'

'Mrs Grey,' Kate said gently, leaning forward, 'we are both mothers and God only knows how it would affect us to lose a child. It must be almost as bad to lose a grandchild, and I imagine all of you must have been beside yourselves with grief. But some of us are stronger mentally than others, aren't we? And tragedy affects us all differently. I can see you're a strong person, and so I expect Billy is too. But Maureen isn't. She can't help that – she just isn't. And, with such unbearable grief, she reacted violently because she had to blame somebody, *anybody* – Billy even.'

'They kept her in Bodmin for six months,' said Mrs Grey. 'But Billy had gone up to London. Money's good up there and there weren't nothin' for him round here, was there? Only me. He stayed here for a while off and on, but we don't get on that well.'

'Sometimes we take out our resentment and sorrow on the person we love most. Perhaps Billy did that to you, and perhaps Maureen took hers out on Billy. I really want to help, Mrs Grey, and I have a long – and possibly fruitless – journey ahead of me. But it's worth a try.'

Mrs Grey eased herself up slowly from the armchair. 'I'll have a look,' she said, heading for the door, 'and find that address for you. Can't remember it offhand.'

Kate could hear much rummaging going on next door before Mrs Grey reappeared with a scrap of paper on which she'd written the address.

'They live in Shoreditch,' she said, handing the scrap of paper to Kate, 'but it's very close to Bethnal Green Tube station. Her name is Delyse Barber. Nassau Road, number 182. It's a flat.'

'Thank you so much,' Kate said, memorising the address in case she lost the piece of paper. 'I'm really grateful to you.'

'She's such a beautiful little girl,' Mrs Grey said dreamily. 'Jasmine, she's called. Looks a lot like her dad, just like Lucy did, God rest her soul. Just make sure that Maureen don't harm her. She went mad once so she could go mad again. Do you want a cup of tea?'

'No thank you, Mrs Grey. I'd love one but I've a long drive ahead of me so I'd best be on my way. But I promise that next time I will! You've been very helpful and understanding. Thanks so much for the address. Wish me luck!'

'I do wish you luck, 'specially if it helps to free my Billy,' Mrs Grey said, her lower lip trembling as she escorted Kate to the door.

Kate turned and gave the other woman a hug. 'I'm going to do my best,' she said.

As she drove away Kate tried to imagine how Mrs Grey must be feeling. It was almost impossible to think of either of her two sons in jail for murders they didn't commit, and she felt her eyes brim with tears. Motherhood was also a life sentence in a strange sort of way.

Four hours and ten minutes later Kate drew up outside Shirley Munro's smart house on the outskirts of Windsor. When Kate had left to live in Cornwall, her friend Shirley's parting shot had been, 'There'll always be a bed for you here!'

'I've come for that bed you promised,' Kate said with a grin as Shirley opened her smart grey-green front door. Grey-green front doors were the thing at the moment and Shirley liked to be with it, right down to her enormous open-plan living/dining/kitchen area, with its bi-fold doors to the courtyard garden and the carefully arranged shabby-chic furnishings.

Like good friends everywhere they exchanged news, jokes and memories, while getting through large quantities of wine and food. At eleven o'clock Kate yawned and said, 'I must go to bed now; I need to be up really early tomorrow. I'm hoping to be back sometime in the afternoon with a woman called Maureen and then we'll drive down to Cornwall.'

23

At nine o'clock on Saturday morning Kate was on a train from Windsor heading towards Waterloo, feeling more nervous than she had in years. What if her hunch was wrong and Maureen *hadn't* gone to Shoreditch? What if Maureen *was* the killer and left the note? *What the hell am I doing up here anyway? Why should I care? Well,* she told herself, *I've got to try. I'll be home tonight, hopefully, with or without Maureen, and Woody need never know I came here. I'll take the note to him on Monday. No, I won't, I'll take the note to him* tomorrow.

She withdrew the note from her handbag as the train was crossing the Thames between Richmond and Kew. How *could* it have been from Maureen? There'd been no signs of any technology in Maureen's house, unless she had a laptop and printer hidden away in her bedroom. Because you couldn't very well ask anyone else to type a note like that out for you.

By the time Kate could see The Shard towering above the rooftops on her right, as the train slid into Waterloo, she was feeling more confused than ever. The worst of the rush hour was over but Kate was still amazed at the sheer volume of people moving at speed in every direction, pulling suitcases along, talking on their phones. She'd forgotten about all this after only a few months in Cornwall and she wondered if she was already becoming a country bumpkin, particularly as the crowds thundered past her down the steps into the Underground.

Kate spent the journey on the Northern Line wedged between the door and a young couple, speaking in some unrecognisable language in between kissing and openly fondling each other. As always she was amused by the complete disinterest of all the other passengers staring vacantly into space, if not on their phones. Fortunately, the Central Line to Bethnal Green was quieter, if less entertaining, and Kate got a seat.

As she surfaced into the daylight, the noise and the traffic, she hesitated for a moment trying to remember the directions to Nassau Road and then checked the map on her phone. She set off past parades of shops selling everything from halloumi to halal meat, mangoes to Marengo, curtains, curries, sari shops, coffee shops and newspapers in every language imaginable. It couldn't be more different to Tinworthy's modest parade of shops. Kate breathed in the exotic sights and smells and smiled to herself. Having only had a slice of toast for breakfast some of these savoury smells were making her mouth water.

Nassau Road was the second turning on the right; a long road of mainly Victorian villas, most of which had been converted into flats, many looking sadly neglected. Number 182 was marginally tidier than some with its three doorbells clearly marked. 'D Barber' was the lower one, so presumably the ground floor.

Kate was desperately hoping that Delyse was in, otherwise she'd have to hang around somewhere until she came back, *if* she came back. Her stress levels going ballistic again for the second time in two days, she pressed the bell. There appeared to be no entry system but, with great relief, Kate heard footsteps approaching from within.

The door opened. The black woman who stood there was statuesque and beautiful. Kate was mesmerised for a moment before saying hesitantly, 'I'm sorry to bother you but I'm looking for a Miss Barber.'

'I'm Delyse Barber, and who are you?' the woman asked, staring hard at Kate.

'I'm Kate Palmer, a friend of Maureen Grey, from Cornwall, and I'm trying to find her.'

The woman continued to stare. 'And what makes you think she's here?'

Kate could now detect a West Indian accent. 'I think she wanted to meet Jasmine,' she said.

The woman's stance relaxed a little. 'Just a moment,' she said, and closed the door again.

Kate waited on the doorstep, now convinced Maureen was inside, and praying that she'd be allowed in. A couple of minutes passed before the door was opened again and the woman said, 'You'd better come in.'

Kate followed her through a glass-panelled door into what was obviously the tiny hallway of the ground-floor flat, off which were four further doors. One of them opened and a little girl appeared. She was a beautiful child, slim and delicately boned, with enormous brown eyes and her hair tied up with a red ribbon into a topknot.

Then a familiar voice called out, 'Don't tell me you've let her in, Delyse?'

Kate entered a sunny sitting room where, next to a table on which stood a half-constructed Lego house, Maureen was sitting.

'Hi, Maureen,' Kate said.

'How the hell did you know I was here?' Maureen asked by way of a greeting.

'I guessed.'

'There's no getting rid of this bloody woman,' Maureen said to Delyse.

The little girl had climbed onto the chair alongside Maureen and was studying some pieces of Lego.

'We're building a house for my doll,' she informed Kate.

'And very nice it is too,' Kate said. 'You must be Jasmine?'

The little girl nodded as she stuck a few more pieces together. 'We need to make another window, Auntie Maureen.'

Auntie Maureen!

'I've come, Maureen, to take you back to Cornwall with me. Tonight.' Kate spoke firmly.

'I'm *not* going!'

'You'd better sit down,' Delyse said to Kate, indicating the settee.

'You *are* Billy's partner, aren't you?' Kate asked.

'Yes. Did you expect a blonde?'

'I didn't expect anything, Delyse. I only hoped to find Maureen before the police did. But thanks for letting me come in.'

Delyse stood silently for a minute. Then: 'Let me tell you something,' she said, pointing at her little daughter, 'if anything should ever happen to her, God forbid, I don't think I'd be able to carry on living. I don't know how Maureen's survived and I didn't even know she existed until a few weeks ago. Don't you think she's been through quite enough?'

Kate hadn't expected this. These two women had apparently bonded in a very short period of time. She looked at Maureen who was silently continuing to construct the wall of Lego.

'The reason I'm here,' Kate said, 'is because if Maureen doesn't come back with me, the police will arrive here eventually and I'm afraid they just might put her back in prison because she wasn't supposed to leave Tinworthy at all. If you come back with me now, Maureen, we can just say you went away for one night to sort yourself out or something, and I'm sure the police won't bother to take it any further. And, Maureen, you *know* Billy didn't commit these murders! And, however gallant it is of him to take the blame so you could be released, it isn't *right*.'

No one spoke. The only sound was the clicking of the Lego bricks.

'The thing is, Maureen,' Kate went on, 'as long as Billy's in custody the police can't justify continuing to look out for someone else. Which means there's at least one killer on the loose out there somewhere. Is it you?'

When Maureen finally looked up, Kate saw that her eyes were full of tears. 'How can you think that? You're supposed to be my friend. I don't want to go back, not yet. I'm happy here, Kate,' she said.

Kate swallowed. 'But you can come back afterwards. You can't do that if they stick you in jail. I've always been pretty sure *you're* not guilty and you said yourself that Billy wasn't guilty, didn't you?'

'Billy's a two-timing idiot but he's not guilty,' Delyse said firmly. 'We need to show the police the proof, Maureen.'

'What proof?' Kate asked.

'He'd come back here the night that woman was murdered,' Delyse said. 'He came to tell me that he was going back to live in Cornwall. We'd had a terrible row before he left because I'd asked him why he wouldn't marry me, for Jasmine's sake if nothing else, and he said he couldn't. No explanation. I didn't know he was married until the police stormed in here.'

'That's Billy for you,' murmured Maureen.

'And once the police told me,' Delyse said, 'I was so upset and angry I didn't care what happened to him. I told them he'd left a week before but didn't tell them he'd come back for one night to get his things.' She sighed. 'He slept on the sofa there.'

'But what proof do you have of that?' Kate asked, trying to make sense of what she was hearing.

'I've got his train tickets,' Delyse replied. 'I found them under the sofa when I was vacuuming. It's got the date on them, and he bought them at Bodmin Parkway station.'

'May I have them?' Kate asked.

There was a further silence for a minute before Kate turned to Maureen. 'We've *got* to prove him innocent – you cannot let him take the blame just because he deserted you all those years ago! He was Lucy's dad, he *is* Jasmine's dad, and why should Jasmine grow up thinking her dad's a murderer?'

'I think she's right, Maureen,' Delyse said as she walked towards the door. 'Let me see where I put the tickets.'

Jasmine continued to build her house – seemingly oblivious to the conversation – but then looked up and said, 'Where are you going, Auntie Maureen?'

Maureen wiped her eyes. 'I promise I'll be back very soon, Jasmine. I'll come up to see you often. Promise.'

Kate was touched and surprised by this other deep bond that seemed to have developed overnight between Maureen and the little girl. Perhaps Maureen had finally found an outlet for her bottled-up maternal love.

Delyse came back into the room and, without further ado, handed several tickets to Kate. 'One of these shows part of his debit-card number too. He must have kept his return one separate. I just don't ever want to see that man again,' she said, 'but neither do I want him to get life for something he didn't do, particularly for Jasmine's sake.'

Kate took the tickets, studied them for a moment, noted the date and the last four digits of the banks card and inserted them carefully into her bag alongside the note. 'Thank you.'

Then a little childish voice piped up, 'Isn't Daddy coming back again?'

It was Maureen who spoke. 'I'm sure your daddy will always come back to see you. And I'm sure he'll be back soon.'

Delyse cleared her throat. 'Sometimes, Jasmine, mummies and daddies can't always be together, but I'm sure your daddy will always be with you whenever he can.'

'That's OK,' said Jasmine with a wisdom beyond her years, 'because everyone in my class has a daddy they only see some-times.'

Delyse rolled her eyes. 'That's twenty-first century Britain for you!' she said, and Maureen smiled faintly.

'Maureen, just one more thing. Did you leave a note on my pillow the night you left?'

Maureen stared at her with an astonished expression. 'A *note*? What are you talking about?'

'Just a thought,' Kate said, 'because somebody did.'

'Well, it certainly wasn't me,' Maureen said.

'I thought not, but you still need to come with me to clear your name and Billy's.'

'OK,' Maureen said, standing up wearily, 'I'll come back with you to Cornwall.'

'So how did you get here?' Kate asked.

'On the train from Bodmin of course,' Maureen replied. 'I got a lift in a delivery truck from Tinworthy. It had been unloading washing machines at the electrical store and the driver lived in Bodmin. I knew him by sight, reckoned he'd be safe enough.'

'No flies on you, Maureen,' Kate said.

There was little conversation between them on either the Tube or the train back to Windsor.

Maureen had never been to Windsor before. 'Will I see the castle?'

'Yes, from a distance,' Kate replied.

There was an almost childlike innocence about Maureen. 'Is this where they play rugby?' she asked as the train pulled into Twickenham and, 'Will we be near the airport?' as a jet roared overhead. It was almost four o'clock before they got back to Shirley's house. Kate refused the offer of a meal although she was, by this time, very hungry.

'We'll stop and have something to eat on the way home,' she told Maureen as they bade farewell to Shirley.

*

'Jasmine's a very bright little girl,' Maureen remarked as they joined the manic traffic on the M4.

'You two got on well, didn't you? Does she look like Billy?'

'Yes, a little bit. She's almost the same age as Lucy was when…'

'It must have been hard for you to meet her then?'

'No,' Maureen said, 'it wasn't. I don't know why but we just hit it off straight away. She's a lovely kid – more like her mother than Billy, thank God. Delyse is a lovely person too.'

'She seemed nice,' Kate agreed, 'and *very* attractive.'

'She's from Jamaica, you know,' Maureen said, 'but she came over here when she was a little girl, not much older than Jasmine is now. I'll never understand why someone who looks like her could have fancied Billy in the first place. I mean, he's not bad-looking but she could have had *anybody*.'

Kate laughed. 'He must have *something*.'

'He has a way with him,' said Maureen, but omitted to mention what that might be.

'Incidentally, Maureen, do you have a computer? A laptop, iPad, anything like that?'

'No,' she replied, 'I don't. I should get one I suppose but I'm not very interested. And I wouldn't have a clue how to use it. Why do you ask?'

'It could transform your life, put you in touch with people, order your stuff online.'

Maureen sniffed. 'Don't think I'll bother.'

'OK, just wondered.' That was proof enough for Kate that Maureen hadn't put the note on her pillow. 'Now I'm not a big fan of motorway service places,' Kate said as they approached the Swindon area, 'so would you mind if we took an exit somewhere and found a nice pub? It's my treat.'

It took a little time to find a suitable pub and, once they were parked, Kate picked up her bag and double-checked to make sure that the note and the tickets were still safely in there. Whoever had deposited that note on her pillow was still at large, but she was now confident it wasn't Maureen.

24

Kate finally got home at half past ten, having stopped off for an hour to eat, and then taking Maureen home to make sure she was all right.

'I'm contacting the police tomorrow,' she told Maureen as they parted company. 'I've several things to tell them.'

She wasn't at all sure if Woody would be on duty on a Sunday. Probably not, but she planned to phone him anyway because this information couldn't wait.

There was no sign of Angie, who was presumably in The Greedy Gull with Luke. Kate felt exhausted. She'd had two frantic days, continuously stressed and apprehensive. But it was all worth it to have persuaded Maureen to come home, and to have possession of Billy's train tickets.

Kate's mind was still going round in circles and she knew she needed to unwind. She poured herself a large glass of Shiraz and she'd only taken one sip when the phone rang. Was it Maureen? What could have happened now?

It wasn't Maureen. It was Des from The Greedy Gull.

'Could you please come and help your sister home?' he asked. 'She's smashed as a rat and looks like she could pass out at any minute.'

'*What?*' Kate's heart was thumping again. 'Where's Luke?'

'No idea,' said Des. 'Sorry to bother you an' that.'

'I'll be along shortly.' Kate was furious. She did *not* need this. What on earth had possessed Angie to get so drunk? And where was that wretched Luke?

Pulling on her jacket she patted an excited Barney on the head. 'No, we're *not* going for a walk,' she said firmly.

She stomped along the lane to the pub which, being Saturday night, was crowded, with drinkers spilling out onto the outside furniture probably for the first time since last year. She prayed Woody wouldn't be there to see her having to drag her drunken sister home. What on earth had got into her – apart from the gin, of course?

Kate pushed her way through the throng towards the bar, looking right and left as she went. She finally got to the front and caught Des's eye. 'She's over on that seat by the window,' he bellowed as he pulled pints.

Pushing her way through the chatting, laughing crowd Kate finally found Angie, slumped on a seat, half asleep and having dropped her glass on the floor. It hadn't broken but its contents had long ago soaked into the carpet and all that remained was a sad slice of lemon.

'*Angie!*' Kate shook her. 'What the hell are you playing at? Come on, wake up!'

Angie half opened her eyes but was having trouble focusing. 'Kate,' she mumbled, 'wanna drink?'

'I do *not* want a drink!' Kate snapped. 'You have to come home – get *up!*'

'Don't wanna…'

'*Get up!*' Kate shouted, and then looked round in embarrassment as several people had turned with interest to see what was going on. A man she'd never seen before came forward and said in a strong Irish accent, 'Would you like me to help you get her to her feet?'

Kate was humiliated but she needed assistance. 'Yes please,' she said and, between them, they got Angie balanced in an upright position.

'Thanks so much,' Kate said. 'She really doesn't make a habit of this.'

'Ah, we all need to let our hair down sometimes. Are you sure you can manage?'

Kate nodded, thanked the man again, put her arm round Angie to support her and half dragged her out of the door and into the cool air, which seemed to wake her up a little.

'Where we going?'

'We're going home,' Kate replied, fervently hoping Angie would stay on her feet until they got to Lavender Cottage. With a great deal of heaving, groaning and muttering, Kate managed to manoeuvre her sister into the sitting room and dumped her onto the armchair like a sack of potatoes.

'You're a bloody disgrace! I've had a long hard day and then I come back to find you completely hammered and making an exhibition of yourself. Where's the wonderful Luke? Has he had enough of you?' Kate was beyond being furious, not to mention being stressed all over and highly embarrassed.

Angie hiccupped. 'Water.'

Kate brought her a glass of water and watched carefully to make sure Angie didn't spill it all over the place.

'So where is he?' Kate persisted. 'And why were you in that state?'

'He's at home,' Angie mumbled, 'with Brett.'

'Who's Brett?'

Angie gulped some more water. 'And he's only eighteen.'

'Who's only eighteen?'

'Brett.'

'Eighteen what? Years? Stones?'

'Eighteen years old. Are you *deaf*?'

Kate took a deep breath and counted to ten. 'So who is eighteen-year-old Brett then?' she asked, having put two and two together and arrived at the conclusion she'd always suspected.

'A boy,' Angie said, letting her head fall back and within a couple of minutes she was fast asleep.

Kate found a blanket, covered her over and climbed wearily up the stairs to bed.

In spite of being exhausted Kate slept badly, unable to wind down, and aware that she still had little idea who the killer might be. She didn't know either how Woody was likely to react to her so-called investigations, not to mention her trip to London. Then she worried about Angie who'd been behaving remarkably well recently due, in all probability, to her friendship with Luke and working in The Gallery. Had Angie not realised that Luke might be gay? Surely she couldn't have thought that a man who was a good twenty years her junior was likely to have romance in mind? These thoughts went round and round in her head like a never-ending whirlpool.

Kate had tied her window shut with a piece of string, which she attached to the bedpost. It wasn't much of a deterrent but at least she'd wake up if anyone tried to open it. All in all it didn't make for a great night's sleep.

When she staggered down to the kitchen at seven o'clock, she found the armchair empty, so Angie had obviously woken up at some point and taken herself to bed. *Thank goodness for that*, Kate thought, *because I really couldn't cope with a miserable hungover Angie as well as everything else.*

She buttered some toast and wondered when she should phone Woody, then decided to leave it until later in the morning. She would dearly love to call at his house but didn't dare. Tongues were already wagging and they were meant to be keeping their friendship low-key.

She finally called Woody on his mobile at half past ten.

'Hi, Kate! Good to hear from you!'

'Are you at home or in the office?'

'I'm still at home,' he said, 'but I should really call in at the station for an hour or two later.' She heard him yawn. 'But until this damned thing is written off completely I have to be available pretty much twenty-four/seven.'

'I need to see you urgently. Shall I come up to the police station?'

'Yes, of course. Come up any time after midday. Are you OK? I *did* tell you to be careful.'

'Yes, I'm fine. Just had a couple of busy days and not a lot of sleep, but I have some important items to show you.'

'Well, bring them along! Incidentally,' he went on, 'you'll be interested to know that your friend Maureen's reappeared. God only knows where she's been.'

'Only God and myself,' Kate corrected him.

Woody – clad in jeans and a roll-neck sweater – was engrossed in the paperwork on his desk when Kate was shown in.

'Hi, Kate, sit down.' He shuffled the papers to one side. 'It's good to see you.'

'I've had an interesting few days,' Kate said, searching carefully in her bag. 'And this' – she chucked the note across the desk to him – 'is what I woke up to, on my pillow, on Friday morning.'

Woody read it, looked up with a puzzled expression, and read it again. 'On your *pillow?*'

'Correct. I have this window that doesn't shut properly and my bed is right alongside it. I like to feel the cool air, you see. Somebody climbed up, leaned through the window and attached it to my pillow with a stonking great hatpin.' Kate burrowed further in her bag, produced the hatpin and rolled it along the desk towards Woody. 'So who would be likely to have a hatpin like that?'

'Dear lord!' Woody was visibly shocked. 'Whoever this was could have killed you, Kate! Why did you not bring this note to me straight away? Why did you wait two days? Kate, this is—'

'Because I went to London to find Maureen and bring her back,' Kate interrupted.

'*What?*' Woody closed his eyes for a moment and then opened them again.

'I went to London to find Maureen and bring her back,' Kate repeated.

'You did *what?*'

Kate grinned at him. 'You heard.'

'I can't quite believe what I'm hearing! How did you know she was in London? Where was she?'

'She was visiting Billy's lady friend and little girl.'

Woody pushed his chair back and gazed up at the ceiling for a moment. When he straightened up he asked, 'And how did you know she was *there?*'

'Don't you remember our conversation in Truro? I said to you then that I could get close to people and that they were more likely to confide in me than in the police.'

Woody nodded silently for a moment, staring at her. 'But how did you know where she lived?'

'I persuaded Billy's mother to give me the address.'

'Is there no end to your talents? But then how did you persuade Maureen to come back?'

'I said it was unfair to let Billy rot in prison when he hadn't killed anyone. Why should that innocent child have to live with the knowledge that her father was a murderer if he wasn't? And I pointed out – more importantly – that meant the real killer was still at large.'

'Kate,' Woody said with a long-suffering-type sigh, 'Billy has *confessed!*'

'I know that. But even you weren't altogether convinced, were you? Yes, he was doing it to get Maureen off the hook, trying to make up for deserting her and all that. And I reckon that, as neither woman now wants him, he doesn't greatly care what happens. And he could hardly have pinned that note to my pillow if he was in jail, could he?'

Woody looked stunned.

'And the person who left the note in my pillow must be the killer,' Kate said. 'Furthermore, he or she must know that I suspect them.'

Woody continued to stare at the note.

'And I have further proof it wasn't Billy,' Kate went on, digging out the rail tickets. 'He was back in London for one night – and one night only – to get his things. The night Fenella was killed. He came back the next day. I have the rail tickets that Delyse found on the floor after he'd left. Great Western, Bodmin Parkway to Paddington: right day, right date.' Kate slid the ticket across to him. 'Last four numbers on the payment card prove they're his.'

Woody picked up the tickets and studied them. 'I suppose,' he said doubtfully, 'they could be *anybody's* tickets, but we can check his payment card.'

'*Anybody's?* Found under Delyse Barber's sofa where he spent the night?'

'So why didn't she show them to the police when they first went round there after the murder?'

'She told me she didn't care what happened to him after she found out about Maureen, so she didn't tell them he'd been back there. She found the tickets later, when she was vacuuming.'

Woody leaned forward. 'Kate, do you have an answer for *everything?*'

'Not quite,' Kate said, 'I'm still not sure who, out of the remaining suspects, the killer might be.'

'Right,' he said, 'I must now call an emergency meeting this afternoon.' He leaned back in his seat and rubbed his eyes. 'In the meantime, I want you to move out of that house into some temporary accommodation. Your life could be in danger.'

'No, it's OK; I've tied the window up with some string so I'd wake up if anyone tried to get in. And I think someone's coming tomorrow to fix it.'

'A piece of *string*!' Woody rolled his eyes. 'Listen, I can't condone anything you've done from a police point of view because of the danger you're putting yourself into. But from a personal off-the-cuff point of view, I think you're crazy – but wonderful!'

Kate laughed and they grinned at each other.

'I'm going to arrange for the guys to go round and work out how whoever it was got up to your bedroom window,' Woody said. 'There may still be a clue there somewhere, because it hasn't rained for a few days, has it? I've no doubt he or she wore gloves but there may be footprints or something. Do you have any ladders lying around outside?'

Kate admitted that they did.

'Well, lock them away. And it's not safe for you to be there, Kate, believe me.'

'The window will be fixed tomorrow,' Kate said firmly, 'and I'll move into the spare bedroom tonight. I'm *not* moving out.'

'There'll be police patrolling the area all night and every night until we catch the killer,' Woody said. 'Now, have you been talking to any of the original suspects lately? Apart from Maureen of course. Could you have upset someone? Seymour Barker-Jones perhaps?'

'No, I only see Seymour occasionally when I walk the dog and we have a chat.' She decided it wasn't a good idea to tell Woody that she'd mentioned her list to Seymour. 'But I think I definitely managed to upset both Sandra Miller and Dickie Payne.' Kate then proceeded to tell him about her afternoon tea at The Atlantic Hotel followed by her visit to the Paynes. 'I'm not Sandra Miller's greatest fan, but she's the fiery quick-tempered type and I can't see her waiting a couple of days to get her revenge. I'm not sure about Dickie Payne though; there's something a little bit menacing about that man.'

'Don't let his weird collection of medical stuff influence you,' Woody said. He withdrew an envelope from a drawer in his desk and placed the note and the rail tickets inside it before placing them carefully into his briefcase. 'Who have you told about this note?'

'No one,' Kate replied truthfully.

'No one at all? What about Angie?'

'No, I didn't tell Angie because I knew she'd likely panic and go running to the police, and then I wouldn't have been allowed to go to London and bring Maureen and the tickets back. So, you see, there was method in my madness!'

'Kate, are you working tomorrow?' he asked.

'Yes, always on Mondays.'

'The moment you've finished can you please come up to the station here and make a formal statement?'

'Of course,' Kate said, 'but on one condition: that you don't go arresting Maureen again if and when you release Billy.'

'Will there be anything else, madam?' There was a touch of sarcasm in Woody's voice although he was smiling.

'Yes, I'd love a cup of coffee.'

25

Kate arrived back at Lavender Cottage to find Angie, still in her dressing gown, peeling potatoes.

'I'm sorry about last night,' she said as Kate came in.

'So you should be. What on earth got into you?'

Angie sighed. 'I was just feeling a bit low. I know I'm past my prime, Kate, but do you think I'm still *reasonably* attractive?'

Kate stared at her sister. 'What's brought this on? Of course you're still attractive! This wouldn't have something to do with Luke, would it?'

'Well, he seems to have gone off me. This Brett has suddenly appeared out of nowhere. He's only eighteen, an art student and apparently Luke used to teach him art at school when he was a kid. Did you know Luke used to be an art teacher?'

'No, I didn't.'

'Now this Brett's looking for a summer job and somewhere to stay and he's moved in with Luke. And he's going to be working with Luke for the next few months.' Angie sniffed noisily. 'I seem to have outlived my attractiveness and my usefulness.'

'I'm sorry about that, Angie. I know you were fond of him. You can't blame yourself though – sounds like this Brett might be more his type, if you see what I mean.'

There was silence except for the *chop, chop, chop* as Angie massacred an onion.

'I've prepared some lamb shanks for our supper later,' she said. 'I'm sorry about last night but I just felt rejected and discarded and unwanted.'

Kate moved across and hugged her sister. 'Angie, you'll never be unwanted or rejected! You just chose the wrong guy. You can't compete with Brett and that's that.'

Angie clung on to Kate. 'I feel a fool. I should have known.'

'You're not a fool, Angie. You're a normal affectionate woman. You'll meet someone else; you've got masses of time yet.'

'I'm nearly *sixty*!' she moaned as she extricated herself.

'Hey, sixty's supposed to be the new forty! Remember what our mum used to say? "What's for you won't go past you" – she was forever saying that.'

'Maybe there's nothing *for* me. And nobody's bought my painting yet.'

'Angie, the season's only just beginning. There'll be hordes of people visiting here in the coming months and I bet someone will buy it.'

Angie blew her nose. 'I hope you're right. Anyway, what have *you* been up to in London?'

'Maureen Grey disappeared and I had a hunch as to where I might find her. And I did.' She gave Angie brief details of her trip. 'More importantly, are you quite sure this guy's coming to fix my window tomorrow morning? And you'll be here, won't you?'

'Yes, I'll be here. He said he'd be here around nine. What's the panic all of a sudden? The window's been like that ever since we moved in and I thought you liked fresh air on your face?'

'Not as much as I used to,' Kate said drily, wondering whether it was wise to inform Angie about the intruder. Bearing in mind that the police might well be calling she decided she'd better. Kate tried to sound matter of fact about it for Angie's sake, but she was feeling more anxious and apprehensive than she cared to admit, even to herself. When she'd finished, Angie sat down on a kitchen chair, ashen-faced.

'You could have been killed! We could both have been killed! Who on earth would do such a thing? Why do they think you know something?'

'I really have no idea,' Kate said.

'It's that bloody list of yours! You've been chasing after the people on it, haven't you? And one of them doesn't like it.'

'That's about it,' Kate agreed. 'I thought I should tell you because the police may call in from time to time, and the scene of crime officers will be arriving soon to look for clues.'

'It could still be my serial killer,' Angie groaned. 'I think he's out there looking for someone else to knife and now he knows where *we* live.'

'For God's sake, Angie, I think I'd know if I'd met some serial killer! Get it into your head – it's someone I've *met*! On the list! Now, isn't it time you got dressed?'

'I'm not sure whether to wear my sackcloth and ashes or my shroud,' Angie said as she got up to go.

Sunday evening or not, two police officers arrived at Lavender Cottage at five o'clock.

'Can we see your ladders, please?' they asked. Kate unlocked the garage, indicated the ladders and left them to it. When she went out later to offer them a cup of tea – which they politely refused – they were able to show her exactly where the ladder had been placed, indicating the two dents in the ground.

'Still got mud on it,' one of them said, showing Kate the foot of the ladder.

Then the other one said, 'Have either of you ladies got big feet?'

Kate had been asked some odd questions in her time but not, until now, the dimensions of her feet.

'No, not really,' she said, stepping forward so that her feet could be seen clearly. 'I'm a size seven, and I think my sister is too.'

'Have you had anyone at all round here in the past few days – workmen, say?'

Kate was puzzled. 'Not that I'm aware of. Why do you ask?'

'Oh, no reason,' the first one said. 'The detective inspector will tell you.'

He certainly will, Kate thought, intrigued.

Woody phoned in the evening after they'd eaten their lamb shanks.

'I just wanted to make sure you were all right,' Woody said. 'I'm worried about you.'

'You've no need to be,' Kate said, 'I'm fine.'

'Well, there'll be a police patrol round at regular intervals,' he said. 'Have you warned your sister?'

'Yes, I have,' Kate said, looking across at where Angie was fortifying herself with an enormous gin.

'I just wanted to make sure you were OK,' he repeated.

'I'm still a little tired but I'm fine,' Kate said.

'I *know* I keep repeating myself, but I want you to be very, *very* careful, Kate. I also know you want to solve this thing single-handed, but please leave it to us now. Just keep a low profile, keep your doors and windows locked and your phone close by. Much as I appreciate the help you've given, this is not the time for you to be out and about alone doing your detective work.'

'OK, I'll be careful – promise!'

'And keep your ladders locked away.'

Her shift at the medical centre the following day proved to be interesting.

A woman with wild, dark, untameable hair and a face full of freckles arrived for a blood-pressure check. Even in this part of Cornwall Kate didn't expect her patients to arrive in wellingtons. But Alyss Evans did.

Inevitably their conversation came round to the murders.

'I hear it was the Greys who did it,' said Alyss eagerly.

'No,' Kate said, 'both Maureen and Billy Grey have been released.'

'So, who do they think it is?' asked Alyss.

'No idea. I suppose it could be Fenella's husband, Seymour Parker-Jones, or Dr Payne or…'

'*Surely* it can't have been that nice Dr Payne! Such a gentleman! He was so kind to my Archie when we first moved in and we thought he had chicken pox. Why on earth do they think it's him?'

'Well,' Kate said, being careful not to go into any details about the doctor's long-running affair with Fenella, 'apparently he hasn't got an alibi for the night of the murder. He was supposed to have gone to Camelford to buy some milk but they can't trace him on the CCTV from Good Buys supermarket.'

'Remind me,' Alyss said, with a look of emerging realisation dawning on her face, 'what night was that murder in the village hall?'

'It was Monday, the twenty-fifth of March,' Kate replied.

'Well, that was *me* who served him! That was the last night I worked there. I'd only gone there for a month temporary, to give us some extra money. And I'd actually left on the Friday but I had to work a shift for Karen Mason, because she'd worked a day for me the week before that. I don't think they changed the names on the rota; they weren't very bothered about things like that as long as the shift was covered. And I remember him!'

'You should go straight to the police with that information,' Kate said.

'I will.'

It now appeared Dickie Payne was in the clear as far as Fenella's murder was concerned. But could he, for some reason, have delivered the note? And why?

*

Mindful of Woody's instructions, Kate made her way up to the police station at half past three and then had to wait almost half an hour because, she was told, the detective inspector was in a meeting.

'Sorry to keep you waiting, Kate,' he greeted her when he eventually emerged. 'Come in.'

He set up the recorder and they got started – his questioning thorough, her answers as concise as she could make them – and the whole thing was done by quarter to five. She'd described her hunch, how she found Maureen, about Delyse Barber, the rail tickets and their return. He informed her that an Alyss Evans had made a statement about Dr Payne that very morning. 'The supermarket insisted we'd spoken to everyone concerned, but they didn't appear to know that Alyss had worked for someone else that Monday.'

'So she wasn't on the rota that evening?'

'Correct.'

When they'd finished Woody said, 'Now, you need to be careful and don't go wandering around on your own.'

'But I need to walk the dog sometimes,' Kate protested. 'Angie's so worried about getting murdered she won't go any further than the pub.' Angie had, in fact, bought some sort of anti-attack spray, which she'd been advised to aim at the face of any assailant, who would then be so overwhelmed with the odour it released that she'd have plenty of time to make her escape.

'Well, let the dog run around in the garden,' Woody advised, 'or else go for a walk in the middle of the village where there's plenty of people around.'

'All right,' Kate agreed, 'but confirm something for me: did my uninvited caller have large feet?'

'Ah yes,' he replied, 'whoever climbed up to your window the other night left a distinct footprint. A large footprint.' He hesitated. 'A *very* large footprint! You really are becoming a super sleuth, aren't you!'

Kate now knew that she'd spend the rest of the week studying everyone's feet and then wondered what possible excuse she could have to visit the Paynes again.

'That should narrow down your list of remaining suspects,' Kate said.

'Hmmm,' said Woody. He was giving nothing away. 'Just be careful, will you?'

Kate arrived home to find the window had finally been fixed and she could dispense with the string. Angie was back in the summerhouse with her art and her anti-attack spray, and Barney was desperate for a walk. Just as she was about to attach the lead to Barney's collar, there was a knock on the door. Kate sighed; who was it *now*?

She opened the door to find Jess Davey standing there, looking agitated.

'You said I could pop in anytime,' Jess said, biting her lip.

'Yes, of course – come in!'

'I ain't disturbin' you?'

Kate shook her head. 'I was only going to walk the dog. He can wait. Cup of tea?'

'No thanks.' Jess hesitated for a moment. 'Oh well, go on then, why not?'

As she made the tea Kate could see that something was bothering the woman. She passed a cup to Jess and sat down opposite her at the kitchen table. 'How's things?'

Jess shrugged. 'I'm a bit worried.'

'About what?'

'Didn't know if I should tell anyone or not.' With that Jess burst into tears.

Kate leaned across and squeezed Jess's hand. 'Tell what?'

Jess took several gulps of tea. 'I've got this package.'

'Don't cry. You can tell me. What package?'

'It's at home,' Jess said, wiping her eyes, 'hidden away. Kevin gave it to me and told me to keep it safe and not give it to anyone.'

'What sort of package? Large? Small? Hard? Soft?'

'Not very big.' Jess made a small round shape with her hands. 'And it's soft.'

'Do you have any idea what's in it?'

Jess shook her head. 'I'm too scared to open it. And Kevin said to keep it safe.'

'Kevin's no longer with us,' Kate said gently, 'and this could be important.'

'So do you think I should take it to the police? It's not as if they was lookin' for it, cos they was only after the phone. Would they be angry cos I didn't tell them about the package before?'

'Of course not; they'll be very grateful.' Kate hoped she was right. Nevertheless she had a gut feeling about this package. 'Do you want me to come with you?'

'No, I'll be OK. You've been very kind. I just wanted your advice. I'll go this evening.' She stood up. 'I'd better go now. Thanks for the tea.'

'Good luck, Jess.'

As Jess cycled down the drive, Kate attached the lead to Barney's collar and trotted down to the beach where there were a few other families with dogs. She found a stick and threw it around for Barney to retrieve, hoping he'd get sufficient exercise that way. She pondered what Jess had said; she had a feeling this package could be very relevant. Then, on the way home, she found herself staring at the feet of every male she met.

And the next morning, in the medical centre, she continued doing just that.

'Have you heard that Billy Grey's been released?' Sue asked when Kate arrived for work.

'Yes,' Kate replied. 'I heard.' Sometime, when this case was finally over, she might tell Sue about her small part in it. She was fond of Sue, who had a heart of gold along with a big appetite for gossip.

'Yes, apparently he's back living with Maureen. Can you believe it? Would you take back a bloke who'd buggered off ten years ago and left you to it?' She didn't wait for a reply. 'So there's still a killer out there and I don't think the police have a cat's chance in hell of ever solving this. Pity really, because that Forrest bloke's very fanciable, but he's already had poor Kevin, Maureen and Billy Grey in custody and we're no nearer knowing who's done it. I tell you now, you won't catch me wandering around on my own anymore when it begins to get dark.'

'Very wise,' Kate murmured.

'And most of the women round here had only just started going out and about again thinking the killer was in prison, so they'll be back barricading themselves indoors again now.'

Every patient had an opinion on this subject.

'I still say it was them two Greys what done it,' old Mrs Barrymore said in between fits of coughing.

'I've always said it was just someone passin' by,' said Arthur Collins as Kate removed the stitches from above his left eye, the result of a recent brawl outside The Tinners. 'No one round here's likely to be killin' like that.'

And so it went on throughout the morning and, as Kate got into her car later, she hoped no one saw her heading towards Higher Tinworthy. Because she had a visit to make.

*

There had been no further requests to visit Clare Payne so Kate knew she'd have to make some excuse to see Dickie, and his feet, again. What might she have left behind? Scissors, perhaps? Worth a try.

Kate knew the doctor drove a blue Audi, which was normally parked in their drive, but there was no blue car in the drive. Should she wait for a few minutes or come back some other time? No, she'd wait. Time was running out.

She decided to park a little further along the road, from where she'd be able to see him driving in – if and when he came back.

Minutes went by. It was very quiet up here. Then Kate heard a car advancing towards her from further along the road and prayed it was the doctor. Instead she saw a sleek black sports car slowing down as it passed. At the wheel was Sandra Miller and, for a brief second, they made eye contact.

Kate shivered as she watched Sandra's car disappear from sight in her rear-view mirror. But then, much to her relief, a blue Audi appeared and turned into the Paynes' driveway. She waited for another few minutes before getting out of her car and heading towards the front door.

'Ah, Nurse Palmer!' Dickie Payne exclaimed as he opened the door. 'I thought it was your red car I saw parked along the road! What can I do for you?'

Not for the first time Kate decided that, when she eventually replaced the Fiat, she'd be wiser to settle for silver or black.

'I'm sorry to bother you,' she said, trying to avoid looking straight at his feet, 'but I wondered if I may have left some scissors behind when I was attending to Mrs Payne. I can't find them anywhere.'

'You'd better come in then,' he said, holding the door wide open.

She forced a smile. 'I really didn't want them incorporated into your impressive collection!'

As he led her into the large sitting room, she allowed herself to look down at his feet which, at first glance, seemed to be of normal size.

'If you wait for a moment I'll check with Clare and the home help,' he said.

Kate seated herself on an extremely uncomfortable but expensively upholstered ottoman and looked round at the immaculate room. Did these two spend their time in this vast formal space? Or did they have a cosy snug somewhere? She hoped they did.

'No scissors have been found,' Dickie Payne announced as he re-entered the room a couple of minutes later.

'Well, thank you for checking,' Kate said as she stood up to go. 'I'm sorry to have bothered you.'

'And,' he added, as he escorted her to the door, 'you may be interested to know that the police have finally located the cashier who served me in the supermarket the night that Fenella Barker-Jones was murdered. She remembered me because we'd met before – when she thought her son had chicken pox.'

'I'm really delighted that's been cleared up,' Kate said truthfully as she walked down the drive. He, or someone, had left a pair of bright green rubber gardening gloves lying on the side of a flowerbed. *Gloves...* suddenly, something clicked into place.

'Likewise,' said the doctor with a trace of a smile.

She glanced again at his feet. They looked to be normal man-sized feet, possibly a size ten or eleven.

Dickie Payne wasn't the killer. Nor was he the note-writer.

Kate was now convinced that the person who left the note wasn't the murderer. She could cross Dickie off her list but she needed to see Seymour Barker-Jones as soon as possible. She was certain Seymour wasn't the killer either, but needed to find out for sure if he'd left the note, and why.

And she was certain she now knew who the killer was.

26

When Kate got home she found the dog, as always, hysterically pleased to see her, and a man standing in the kitchen. It was a man she vaguely recognised and it took her a few seconds to work out who he was. Then she remembered – the kind Irishman who'd helped her when Angie had drunk herself semiconscious over the Luke business. She hadn't had a chance to study him at the time, but she studied him now. In fact, he looked rather nice and – judging by the expression on her sister's face – Angie thought so too. It was then Kate realised that Angie was sitting with her foot up on a stool while the man was asking, 'Where did you say the teabags were?'

'They're in the box marked "Cornish Biscuits", Fergal,' said Angie. 'One of these days we'll get coffee, tea and sugar jars like everyone else. Oh, hi, Kate! This is Fergal. Fergal this is the sister I was telling you about.'

The man called Fergal turned round and beamed at Kate. He had mischievous blue eyes and black hair greying at the temples. 'Hello, sister she's been telling me about!' He held out his hand. 'Fergal Connolly. I have a feeling we met briefly a couple of days ago.' And he gave Kate a deliberate wink.

Kate, feeling ashamed, shook his hand, looking from one to the other in astonishment, noting that Angie was blissfully unaware of this earlier encounter.

'So now you're going to be asking me what on earth I'm doing in your kitchen,' said Fergal, triumphantly waving some teabags in the air, 'and Angela there is about to be telling you!'

Angela indeed! Kate waited, on edge. How soon could she go out without appearing rude?

'Well, I took Barney for a walk down to the village,' Angie said, 'and it started to rain.'

'Oh, it did,' Fergal agreed. 'It just poured.'

Kate sighed, took off her coat and sat down.

'And I suppose, because it's been so dry for a while, that it made the pavement very slippery,' Angie went on.

'Oh, it was,' Fergal confirmed.

'And so I went arse over tit,' Angie said. 'I think I might have tripped over Barney's lead, but I hit the pavement and then slid along for quite a bit with my ankle buckled under me.' She shook her head sadly at the memory of it.

'Just look how swollen it is,' Fergal said, pointing at the ankle.

Kate couldn't actually see much swelling.

'And Fergal was just coming out of the gift shop,' Angie continued, 'and helped me onto my feet.'

'I did. I have this talent for helping ladies to their feet. Now, can I make you a cup of tea?' he asked Kate.

'Well, that's very kind of you, Fergal, but—'

The rain was now lashing against the window. Would Seymour be there?

'Oh, no problem, Kate. Don't suppose you have a box marked "Biscuits", do you?' This remark caused both he and Angie to dissolve into gales of mirth.

Kate stood up. 'Really, that's so nice of you but you must sit down and let me do the honours. Are you here on holiday?'

Fergal relinquished his catering duties and sat down opposite Angie while Kate finished off making everyone's tea and managed to unearth a few custard creams.

'Oh no,' he replied, 'I sell maps and postcards and things. Tourist stuff, you know? And I'd just come out from a couple of your shops when this woman lands at my feet!' More gales of laughter. 'But,' he continued, 'she'd got it in her head that I might be some sort of killer and then of course I remembered that this was the place where they had those murders. I had to practically strip to let her see I wasn't carrying any knives or anything.'

'I *fell* for him in a big way!' Angie was beaming. 'And you practically had to *carry* me home, didn't you, Fergal?'

'Oh, I did indeed. She said I was worth a cup of tea but, because she couldn't stand up for long, I'd have to make it myself.'

Having established that Fergal took milk and sugar, Kate delivered the tea and wondered how to make her exit. She remained standing and said, 'So have you come all the way from Ireland?'

'Oh goodness no! I'm working for a company in Plymouth. Just looking around for new stockists.'

'Including Lower Tinworthy?' Kate asked as she passed him a custard cream.

'Well, I'd not been here before so I thought it was time I familiarised myself with the area and any likely stockists. I've got a couple of them interested, so it's been a good day, and I'll be back.' He grinned at Angie.

'You've been very kind.' Kate said, 'Would you like to stay for supper? It's nothing fancy, just chilli.'

'Oh, I *love* chilli,' said Fergal, 'but I've to meet our district manager at seven tonight back in Plymouth so I should really be on my way soon. And my car's still down in the car park. But I tell you what, I could come back at the weekend. How about Saturday, Angela? We could go out for a meal if you fancied it? And you too,' he added hurriedly, turning to Kate.

'That's kind of you, Fergal, but I have plans for Saturday,' she said. She didn't have plans for Saturday, not yet anyway, but these two seemed smitten with each other already and she had no intention of playing gooseberry.

He then talked nonstop about his job, the maps, guide books and the postcards, the flat he was buying in the Barbican area and, not least, the ex-wife who'd taken all his money and gone off to the States with a man half her age.

'Well, it's been grand talking to you,' he summed up as he drained his tea and bade them both a cheery goodbye. As Kate showed him to the door he said quietly, 'Not a word now about the pub the other night! No need for Angela to know!'

Then, loudly: 'See you Saturday, then!' And he was gone.

'You certainly know how to pick them,' Kate said as she came back into the room. 'Just make sure this one doesn't have you flogging his postcards for him, and without pay.'

'Oh, don't start lecturing me,' said Angie, getting to her feet and heading towards the gin.

'I thought you couldn't put any weight on that ankle?'

'Ah well, it's not *that* bad really, but I just fancied leaning against him as we tottered up the lane. And he's very tasty, don't you think?'

Kate collapsed into the chair. 'You can pour me one while you're at it. It's been quite a day, *Angela*.'

And the worst might be yet to come, she thought.

She finished the gin in three swallows, striving to find some Dutch courage.

Angie looked at her in amazement. 'You don't normally drink like that – what's wrong with you?'

'I'm just feeling tense and needed something to calm my nerves,' Kate replied. 'I'm going to take Barney for a walk.'

'There's no need to take him; he's already had a walk with me. And it's vile out there – bucketing rain and misty.'

Kate ignored her, donning her hooded raincoat and wellington boots. 'Could I borrow your anti-attack spray?' she asked.

'Kate, what *is* this? Where the hell are you going?'

'I told you – I'm taking Barney for a walk, and I need to get out for a bit as well.'

Ignoring Angie's protestations, she pocketed the spray and then, attaching Barney's lead, she set off. She looked at her watch. It was five thirty. Seymour was usually near the bench at about six o'clock. She had time. She was certain he'd be there.

As she crossed the bridge, she had that eerie feeling of the hairs rising on her skin that told her she was being followed. She looked round but the sea mist had descended lower so she could only see a few yards behind. She knew that she wasn't supposed to go anywhere on her own, that she'd been told to stay where there were people around, but even though there were so many visitors everywhere, Kate was confident that the only other person who would brave the cliffs today, in this weather, would be Seymour.

The low cloud had obscured any sea view and only the grey waves crashing against the black rocks immediately underneath were visible and audible. The slope was slippery in places and she had to take care not to skid, wishing she'd worn her walking boots. Even as she climbed up the cliff path she still had that slightly eerie feeling that there was someone following, which was ridiculous on a day like this. Even though her common sense told her otherwise, the feeling was growing, now exacerbated by a cold sensation at the back of her neck. She kept walking, increasingly unwilling to look round, telling herself that she'd seen one too many TV dramas. The imagination could play countless tricks.

Barney continued to run around hither and thither but hadn't yet been joined by any other dogs. Nevertheless, she was beginning to feel a little afraid. This was, without doubt, an impulsive action on her part. She'd disobeyed Woody's instructions to stay safe, not to go off on her own. And now here she was, in the mist and the gloom, doing just that. She mustn't let her imagination run away with her though because who, in their right mind, would be tailing her today? Apart from Angie, no one could know that she was likely to be coming up here. Unless someone was watching her every move?

But that feeling of being followed wouldn't go away. Kate quickened her step and her heart beat a little faster.

And then, ahead of her in the mist, she saw the seat. And Seymour with his dogs. She guessed right; he was there. Now that she knew who the killer was, she needed to find out from Seymour if and why he'd pinned that note to her pillow.

'Hello!' she said. 'Not a very nice day, is it?'

'No,' he said solemnly as she seated herself beside him. 'It certainly isn't.'

When he turned to face her she thought there was something in his look that she'd not seen before. Perhaps she'd been wrong? She felt a tiny frisson of fear. Maybe her *theory* was wrong?

'I was hoping you'd show up,' he said, 'I've been waiting for you.'

It was then she looked down at his boots. Why had she never noticed before how *enormous* they were, how *gigantic* his feet were? *Oh God*, she thought. *Woody will kill me, if Seymour doesn't kill me first.* She sat silently, paralysed with fear for a moment, her hands in her pockets automatically searching for the phone that she'd forgotten to bring with her. At least she had the anti-attack spray.

'Why?' she asked, trying to keep her voice from wobbling. 'Why are you spying on me?'

'Because you've been doing a lot of meddling, haven't you?' He continued gazing out at the almost invisible sea.

Kate gulped. 'Why do you think that?'

'I've been watching you for quite some time,' he said conversationally. 'I find you rather interesting, and very nosy.'

'I'm not nosy,' Kate said.

'Yes,' he said with a sigh, 'you are. But why are you so involved with the Greys? They were, after all, the obvious assailants. Why were you so convinced they weren't the killers? Why are they both free now, Mrs Palmer? Why have the police been at your house? Why have you become so friendly with the detective? I suspected last time I saw you that you could be trouble.'

In spite of her fear Kate was annoyed. 'Who I choose to associate with is my business,' she snapped, 'and nothing whatsoever to do with you.'

He moved a little closer, his arm now touching hers. She shuddered involuntarily.

'Oh, it has a lot to do with me,' he said.

She prayed someone, anyone, would come along the coastal path. But it had begun to rain more heavily again and so that now seemed increasingly unlikely. She looked around for Barney, who was still romping with the two dogs.

'There's no one around,' he said, as if reading her thoughts, 'just you and I.'

'I'm not afraid of you,' Kate said, trying not to shake and wondering how on earth to make her escape. She was younger than him and hopefully she could run faster.

'Why should you be?' he asked.

'Because it was you who left the note on my pillow, wasn't it?'

He didn't answer.

Kate again began to wonder if her theory was wrong. She reckoned they were only nine or ten feet from the edge of the cliff. And oblivion. She was going to have to make a run for it. She looked around in the misty gloom. She'd be safest to go back the way she came because she wasn't too sure where some of these other paths led to – surely if she got back in sight of the village she'd be safe?

'I *know* you left that note on my pillow,' she said.

'Why are you so certain?'

'Because the police have your footprint.' Kate looked down again at his enormous feet.

He smiled and said, 'I never was much good at field work.'

'I never believed you killed your wife and Kevin, but did you?'

He looked at her in amazement. 'No, Mrs Palmer, I didn't kill either of them. I *loved* my wife so why would I have wanted to kill her? But I was outside the door when I heard her arguing with Kevin Barry. He'd gone to prison for her, and she was refusing to pay him.'

'Couldn't you have paid him yourself?'

'Yes, I would have done but I didn't get the chance. We were making arrangements that night at The Tinners when Fenella was murdered. You may not be aware but I have a very important and respected position at Westminster and I wanted this whole thing to be settled and off the front pages. I cannot afford to have scandal in my life.'

'So you didn't kill Kevin either?'

'Of *course* I didn't kill Kevin. I can't pretend I'm sad he's dead but I haven't killed anyone, believe me.'

'I believe you, but then why stick that note on my pillow?'

'Because you've been stirring things up and I need you to stop. I need you to stop defending the Greys when it's plainly *they* who are guilty. And I want them charged so I can get back to London. Do you understand, Mrs Palmer?' Then he stood up and called for the dogs. 'I hope that, if we meet again, it will be in more convivial circumstances.' And, with that, he disappeared into the mist.

Kate had gambled on her theory being right, and it was. She was now in no doubt as to who the killer was. It was then that the weird feeling came back again – that she wasn't alone.

Barney began barking and making a bit of a fuss, and Kate realised that someone else was emerging from the thickening mist.

'I thought he was *never* going to go,' Sandra Miller said.

27

'What do you want?' Kate asked, but she knew. *Of course.*

'I've been waiting for this moment,' Sandra said and sat down beside her.

'You've been following me.' Kate was beginning to feel sick in the pit of her stomach.

'Yes, I've been following you ever since I saw you parked in Higher Tinworthy. *Watching.* Couldn't believe my luck, you coming up here on a day like this. Now there's just you and me, in the mist. So easy to fall over the edge in this weather, happens all the time. Afterwards they'll probably petition to erect a fence.'

'Afterwards?'

'After you *accidentally* fall over the edge.'

Kate began to feel real terror. This woman was mad; she was also younger and probably stronger. She was definitely going to have to make a run for it this time.

Sandra seemed to sense what she was about to do and Kate felt something sharp piercing her coat and tickling her ribs.

'Don't try anything clever, Kate. I really don't want to cut you up. Such a messy business.'

Barney seemed to sense the change in the atmosphere, becoming restless and running to and fro as if to say, 'Come on, we need to go!' *Oh Barney,* Kate thought, *will you be able to find your way home? Will she kill you too?* For the first time her eyes brimmed with tears. Was this to be her last day on earth? There was little chance of escape now with this knife touching her skin, but she had to try something. At least play for time.

'Why did you kill them, Sandra?' She had difficulty speaking; her mouth was so dry that her lips were sticking to her teeth.

'Even you must know that that cow has been having it off with my husband for a very long time.'

'But why wait until *now* to get your revenge?'

'I waited for Kevin Barry to come out of prison because I knew he'd be the main suspect. Then I heard Billy Grey was back on the scene, and it was coming up to the ten-year anniversary of Lucy's death. It was a good time.'

'But why Kevin? What had *he* done to upset you?'

'He saw me killing Fenella, the bastard. He'd come out for a fag, saw me going round from the front door of the hall to the kitchen door, and followed me. He saw everything. Then he said he'd get rid of the apron and gloves for me because I couldn't risk putting them in the bin and certainly not shoving them in my bag in case we got searched. Kevin said he'd burn them for me but the bastard kept them and then of course he wanted money to keep quiet. But he wasn't going to be getting any of mine. And now, Kate Palmer, it's *your* turn.'

'So why kill her in the village hall of all places?' Kate tried to keep her voice from wobbling but she knew only too well that her fate was sealed now that Sandra had confessed to the murders. She twisted a little and immediately felt the knife penetrate her skin. She desperately needed to play for more time.

Sandra gave a snort. 'I'd have finished her off at home. Ida Tilley goes to bed early so that wouldn't have been a problem. But Seymour had suddenly come back.' She paused. 'That night at the WI was deadly – I was bored witless listening to that old crone rabbiting on about her bloody vegetables, so I went out front for a fag and then had a wander round to the kitchen door to see who was in there. And there was Fenella slicing her sodding cake! I decided I might as well give her a hand; she insisted I put on an apron and gloves. I'm allergic to them gloves they've got there and when I refused do you know what she said to me? She said, "You smell like a filthy ashtray!" So I blew my smoky breath in her face and said, "When it comes to filth you're the expert."'

Sandra turned round to Kate and narrowed her eyes. 'Do you know what she said then?'

Kate shook her head.

'She said, "I think of myself as a therapist, darling, helping those unfortunate enough to get little satisfaction from their frumpy wives." It was the way she said "darling" in that posh voice of hers – that's when I saw red. I'm not frumpy and I'm bloody good in bed! Fenella laid the knife down then, so I put the bloody gloves on, picked it up and stabbed her with it. Job done!'

Kate looked round in desperation but the mist had descended again so, even in the unlikely event of anyone being around, they probably couldn't be seen. She could shout, but Sandra would probably silence her with the knife.

For the moment she had to let Sandra think she'd already accepted her fate and had no intention of escaping – in the hope she wouldn't push that knife any further in. She could already feel the pain and the dampness of the blood seeping through her sweater. Kate thought of her two sons. She was probably never going to see them again, and what would they think about their mother being murdered on a Cornish clifftop? She thought of Angie then; would Angie stay on in Lavender Cottage by herself? And she thought of Woody, and how she'd disobeyed all his warnings. Deep down, she'd hoped that they might have had some sort of future together. But now…

Sandra said, 'So we've had our little chat, Kate Palmer – can we just get on with it?'

She placed her left arm round Kate's shoulders and continued holding the knife against her ribs with her right hand, slowly getting to her feet and taking Kate with her.

It was now or never.

Kate, with every ounce of strength she could summon, managed to shove Sandra away, fumbling in her pocket to locate the anti-attack spray. She pulled it out and aimed it at Sandra's face but immediately Sandra knocked it out of her hand.

Kate began to run and run, to run for her life, the dog sprinting alongside, only too aware that this madwoman was thundering after her.

And then she fell. The ground was so slippery that she skidded for several yards before she finally fell in an undignified heap, barely registering the graze on her knee. What did a grazed knee matter when she was about to die? She rolled herself into a ball and waited for the knife to penetrate somewhere. She was past being terrified.

But nothing happened. She lay there waiting for death, knowing there was no escape now. Instead someone was talking to her. A man.

Was she still alive?

Kate slowly tried to raise herself up, only to see Sandra a few feet away writhing on the ground, having dropped the knife.

And there, alongside a uniformed policeman, stood Woody, the Taser still in his hand.

'Cuff her,' he ordered, and the policeman headed towards Sandra with a set of handcuffs. Sandra – even in a diminished state – was having none of it and started trying to kick, necessitating Woody to grab her while the officer clipped on the cuffs. Another officer appeared from the gloom and, between them, the two policemen escorted a swearing, snarling Sandra down the hill.

Kate started shivering, her teeth chattering, the tears flowing.

Woody bent down beside her. 'Kate,' he said gently, 'did she hurt you?'

Kate, between sobs, said, 'I think she's cut me a little, but I'm OK.'

'Thank God,' said Woody, helping her to her feet and then holding her loosely. 'Can you walk a little, Kate? Are you sure?'

Kate nodded dumbly. Then she noticed the policewoman who'd come up behind him.

'This is PC Mandy Williams,' Woody said. 'Mandy's car's at the bottom of the hill and she's going to take you to the medical centre. I'd like to come with you but I have to deal with our friend here. But I'll come up to see you later. Are you sure you're OK to walk down? You're injured and you're in shock.'

Kate began to get her shaking under control. 'Yes, I'm OK. But how did you know…?'

'Angie rang me. She was worried,' he said, stroking her cheek.

28

Kate looked across the table into the deep brown eyes of the man who'd saved her life. They were dining at The Edge of the Moor again, not because they needed to hide their friendship anymore but because they both liked it there so much. Perhaps it was too early to think about love but she hadn't felt anything like this for a very long time. It wasn't that she was looking to marry again, but nonetheless she felt sure they had some sort of future.

As they sipped their drinks Woody said, 'When did you know it was Sandra Miller?'

'I think the penny started to drop the day I took Angie to tea at The Atlantic Hotel, and after that it was a process of elimination.'

'What gave her away?'

'It was the gloves and apron she was wearing that day at the hotel when she emerged from the kitchen. I remembered she had a rash at the quiz, and she could easily have put gloves on and helped Fenella cut the cake. But why agree to wear them if she was allergic? Because, wearing those, she'd have no blood on her, so she could have come back into the hall and made out that she'd only popped out for a cigarette. And there'd be no evidence to give her away. I saw how quickly she could peel off that apron and gloves and roll them up into a ball – easy to get rid of. And no doubt Kevin *kindly* offered to get rid of the evidence for her, for a price. It was when Jess described the package to me that I began to put two and two together. After what you told me about the barman from The Tinners seeing Kevin and Sandra outside together, it occurred to me that if Kevin had witnessed Sandra killing Fenella, it would be a compelling motive for Sandra to murder him. Nobody else seemed to have a strong enough motive for Kevin's murder.'

'So you were convinced it wasn't either of the men?' Woody raised a questioning eyebrow.

'Yes, I was pretty certain neither of the men were guilty of the murders. Dickie Payne was too devoted to his wife to risk abandoning her to serve a jail sentence and then of course he finally had an alibi. And why would Seymour suddenly take against Fenella's love affairs when he'd known about them for so many years? But once you told me about the footprint, I simply had to know who'd put the note on my pillow, and why…'

The waiter hovered while they made their choices from the menu.

After he'd taken their orders Woody said, 'When Angie phoned to say you were "up to something" – that you'd taken her anti-attack spray with you on a horrible evening when the dog didn't really need a walk – I guessed straight away you'd gone up to Penhallion to see someone.' He sighed. 'Kate, do you *ever* do what you're told?'

She grinned. 'But I *needed* to see Seymour to ask why he'd left that note.'

'To confirm that he wasn't the killer?' Woody asked.

'No, by then I was sure he wasn't the killer.'

'So, when you went up on the cliff you didn't think there was any risk?'

'I was pretty certain there was no risk – but then I didn't expect Sandra Miller to have followed me up there.'

Woody picked up his glass and took a large gulp of wine. 'So, did you get a satisfactory answer from Seymour about the note?'

'Yes. He wanted me to stop meddling so that the whole thing would be settled and off the front pages. I did have a few scary moments wondering if I'd got it wrong and he *was* the killer, but everything seems so much more sinister in the mist, don't you think?'

'It certainly makes a favoured setting for scary movies,' Woody said, eating an olive.

'He'd been spying on me from across the valley and had worked out which bedroom was mine.' She shivered. 'Then I had this feeling I was being followed up there but I couldn't be sure. I realised I'd forgotten my phone but I did have the anti-attack spray in my pocket and reckoned I could deal with anything.'

'You underestimated Sandra Miller.'

Kate nodded. 'I did.'

'We just got the result of the analysis of the contents of the package which you guessed rightly contained the plastic apron and gloves. Both had blood on the outside that matched Fenella's. And the gloves had skin cells *inside*, which matched Sandra's DNA.'

'So do you reckon that was another of Kevin's bargaining tools for extracting money, along with the recording on his phone?' she asked.

'Exactly that.'

'Poor Jess. I don't think she had a clue what was in that package. She was only worried because they'd broken the law in the first place by Kevin taking the rap for Fenella and then because she hadn't handed in the package sooner. She was still protecting him even after his death. And do you know what I find incredibly sad about this whole business?' Kate asked.

'No, but I have a feeling you're going to tell me.'

'What's sad is that Seymour truly loved Fenella but perhaps couldn't satisfy her, and so he understood her need to have affairs. And I'm beginning to think that she loved him too but needed to prove to herself that she was attractive sexually. Everyone was so keen to judge her, but not Seymour. And no one's been pointing the finger at the married men she took up with, have they? Why was it all *her* fault? I feel so sorry for her and for them both.'

'She could still have paid Kevin that money though, couldn't she?'

Kate sighed. 'Yes, I suppose she could. I didn't say she was an *angel*!'

The food arrived.

'I'm retiring at the end of the month,' Woody said as he dug into his steak, 'so, if you ever feel the need to solve any more crimes, I'll be right there to offer my expertise.'

Kate laughed. 'I think Tinworthy's had more than its share of crime.'

Their eyes met and lingered for a moment.

'You can never be sure,' he said.

A LETTER FROM DEE

Dear Reader,

Thank you so much for reading *A Body in the Village Hall* and I hope you enjoyed meeting Kate Palmer, amateur sleuth. She's liable to pop up again before long so, if you'd like to keep up with this, or any of my books, you can sign up on the following link:

www.bookouture.com/dee-macdonald

Your email address will never be shared and you can unsubscribe at any time.

If you enjoyed *A Body in the Village Hall*, I'd appreciate it if you could write a review because I love to know what my readers think and your feedback is always invaluable. And you can get in touch via Facebook and Twitter.

Dee x

 AuthorDeeMacDonald

@DMacDonaldAuth

ACKNOWLEDGEMENTS

I must thank my two wonderful editors at Bookouture, Lucy Dauman and Natasha Harding, for their encouragement, advice and endless patience – particularly Lucy who has been involved in the editing of this particular book and could not have been more helpful.

Thanks, as always, to my lovely agent, Amanda Preston, at LBA Books, and to Rosemary Brown for her invaluable help yet again, particularly for her assistance in shaping the plot of this novel. (It's high time Rosemary wrote a book herself!)

Thanks to my husband, Stan, for not interrupting me while I slaved over a hot laptop, and to my son, Daniel, and his family, for their encouragement and for constantly checking my reviews.

Finally, a thousand thanks to the amazing Bookouture team: Kim Nash, Noelle Holten, Alex Crow, Jules Macadam, Hannah Deuce, Hannah Bond, Ellen Gleeson, Alexandra Holmes and my cover designer, Tash Mountford. Many apologies to anyone I've unwittingly omitted. You really are a terrific team!

Made in the USA
Coppell, TX
02 September 2021

61703165R00132